BRINGING
BOOMER HOME

TERENCE O'LEARY

Swan
Creek
⌖Press

This book is a work of fiction. Names, characters, places, and incidents either are products of the author's imagination or are used fictitiously. Any resemblance to actual events or locales or persons, living or dead, is entirely coincidental.

For Peggy and Ed

In memory of Sgt. Merlin German, USMC

1985-2008

CHAPTER 1

Cody couldn't breathe. After the vicious hit, the defensive end pinned him to the turf. He tried to push off the overpowering weight, but he didn't have the strength. Suddenly, a huge hand grabbed the linesman's shoulder pads and tossed him like a rag doll to the field.

"You OK, Little Bro?" Boomer asked.

Cody's chest expanded as he sucked in a deep breath of air. Boomer leaned over him with his face partially concealed by his football helmet and hidden by the shadows cast by the overhead stadium lights. Cody could see his brother's eyes filled with worry.

He didn't answer. He extended his hand. Boomer pulled him to his feet. Jogging back to the huddle, Cody stole a quick glance at the scoreboard. He wasn't worried about the points. They were down by five. A touchdown would still win the game, but they only had time for one more play. One more play against their archrival Panthers. Their season wasn't built on how many games they won, the only thing that mattered was if they beat the Panthers. That, and the fact that this was the last high school football game he would play with his brother, made Cody want to take a time-out and make it last a lifetime.

The tight end ran the play in from the Coach. Cody called the play in the huddle, but he knew it didn't matter. The real play would depend on how the defense set up. The goal-posts seemed like miniature toothpicks across the field. He wiped his sweaty hands on his pants. His heart was pounding so hard that it hurt. He slid his hands under the center and surveyed the defense. He knew it was going to be a blitz. He stepped away from the center and motioned his running back to stay in and block. Back under the center, his voice broke as he tried to bark out the count. He gripped the football and started to back away. Rising up for the block, the center's heel stepped on top of Cody's foot. He stumbled. Falling, he managed to pivot and get his hand down to keep his knees from touching the turf. The running back blocked one of the blitzing linemen.

Cody scrambled. Time slowed down. He felt like he could see every player on the field. The wide receiver streaked down the sideline. Cody rolled with him.

He could hear the defensive end coming up on his blind side. Instinctively every muscle in his body tightened for the impact. Boomer charged in front of him. He heard the deafening collision of two mammoth bodies.

The wide receiver pulled away from the Panthers safety. Cody planted his back foot and threw the ball as hard as he could. He lost it in the stadium lights, then watched it spiral back to earth. The wide receiver and the Panthers safety together looked back over their shoulders. The Panthers safety slowed and the under thrown football drifted into his hands.

Cody collapsed to one knee. He wanted to scream to drown out the cheers from the Panthers bleachers that echoed in his football helmet.

Boomer grabbed his brother's shoulder pads and yanked him to his feet.

"Come on, Little Bro."

Cody tugged off his helmet. He couldn't meet Boomer's eyes. He felt like someone pulled a pin and all the air had left his body. He struggled to put one foot in front of the other. When he reached the sideline the flash from the camera blinded him. When his vision returned he saw Kim, the girl with the camera.

In the locker room shower, the steam was thick as fog. Cody let the cascading water mask his face and feelings. The disappointed and frustrated crash and smash of his teammates' fists and helmets against lockers had stopped. What voices that were left were subdued and then finally silent. He dried off, then wrapped the towel around his waist. The locker room was empty except for boy-man giant sitting on the bench. Cody walked down the aisle and collapsed next to his brother.

"You're only a sophomore," said Boomer. "Next year you're going to be so frigging tough."

"You won't be here next year." Cody rubbed his bruised ribs. "I wanted this game so bad. I wanted us to win." Pain and frustration coated his words, "I screwed up. If only I let the ball go a second sooner."

Boomer's massive hand massaged the back of Cody's neck.

"Whoa. Where's this coming from? How many times have I told you, you never get down on yourself?" Boomer squeezed the back of Cody's neck and gently shook his head. "You played a great game. That's what I'll remember." Boomer groaned as he pushed up from the bench. "Get dressed. Let's get out of here."

They walked together across the deserted high school parking lot. The fire-engine-red Ford F-150 truck gleamed under the stadium lights. Cody tossed his bag in the back of the truck then sat in the passenger seat. Boomer pulled his towel from his bag. He wiped off gravel dust that settled on the truck, his face mirrored in the shiny hood.

Boomer got in and started the truck, then pulled out of the lot. His head was round like a pumpkin, his hair cropped short, his ears seemed too small for such a large head and his nose was slightly bent from being broken more than once. When at ease, his natural expression was a slightly tilted up smile with a boyish inquisitiveness reflected in his brown eyes. He wasn't really a giant, but at 6 foot 5 and 260 pounds, he seemed that way when he walked the high school halls.

Cody powered down the window. The cool autumn breeze couldn't blow away his feeling of despondency, nor could the tires humming on the two-lane asphalt country road as the high school lights retreated into the background. He could still see the football falling short into the Panthers safety's hands and hear the cheers that weren't for him and Boomer.

Cody shook his head and mumbled, "Shit."

"Let it go."

Cody stuck his head out the window. The wind blew tears from his eyes.

The truck's headlights illuminated the stop sign. Instead of turning left for home, Boomer turned right.

"Where're you going?" asked Cody.

"You need to chill."

The country road followed the bends of the river that led to the small town of Grand Rapids. Most of the stores lining Main Street were closed, and tonight the town seemed as subdued as Cody's feelings. A few cars were parked in front of O'Malley's bar, and at the Dairy Queen at the end of the block. Boomer stopped at the flashing stoplight, then drove into the darkness at the edge of town.

Boomer slowed, then turned onto the gravel road leading down to the rapids. He turned off the headlights and drove by feel, pebbles crunching under the tires.

The harvest moon bathed the rapids with ashen hues. Boomer turned off the engine. "Come on." He didn't wait for Cody to follow.

Cody slipped going down the steep embankment. He dug the sides of his shoes into dirt, then jumped the final few feet to the riverbank.

Boomer was already in the river jumping from one rock to the next. A large granite outcropping rose up from the water a third of the way across the river. Boomer jumped and grabbed the edge, then hauled himself up to the flat surface. He sat on the edge, then looked back at his brother.

Cody strained to see the rocks beneath the surface of the rapidly flowing water. The first time he saw Boomer go out to Buffalo Rock, he really thought his brother could walk on water. In spring, when Walleyes run, the rocks are completely submerged by melting winter snow. But in summer and fall, when the water level falls, if you knew where to look, you could see the stepping stones. He jumped to the first rock and felt cold water seep into his gym shoe. He skipped to the next one. Now both shoes were wet. A cloud passed beneath the moon and suddenly it was like he was wearing dark sunglasses. He stood still waiting for moonlight to return while listening to the river.

Boomer reached out his hand. Cody locked his hand around his brother's forearm and Boomer lifted him up to the boulder. They sat side by side with their legs dangling over the edge. Cody fell under the spell of rippling water. The riverbanks were lined with tall trees that stood like dark silent sentinels. Beyond the rapids were islands in the stream and the distant glow of a city where the river merged with the lake. A breeze stirred and trees rustled. Cody inhaled the river's primeval scent of mud and decaying leaves. He rested back on the boulder, cupped his hands under his head and tried to see stars through moonlight.

CHAPTER 2

"Cody. Breakfast's ready."

Cody pressed the pillow against his ear trying to drown out his mother's voice. His body ached. Not just from last night's game, but from the accumulation of countless hits over the season.

"Cody, it's getting cold."

He slid his feet to the wooden floor, pushed upright and cradled his head between his hands. His knees popped as he stood then ambled to the bathroom.

Cody went downstairs and took his seat at the table across from Boomer. His father, Jack, sat to his right. You could say Boomer looked like Jack when he was 18 or Jack was Boomer 22 years in the future.

Eileen placed a plate brimming with pancakes in front of Cody, then added a large glass of orange juice. Boomer favored his father, but Cody looked more like his mother. At 6 foot 1 and 180 pounds, Cody didn't have his brother's bulk or strength. Boomer's face was round, Cody's was more oblong. Cody had his mother's blue eyes and like his mother, his features, ears, nose, chin, and eyebrows were more symmetrical.

Cody's stomach woke up. He smothered his pancakes with butter and syrup.

"Where to today?" asked Boomer.

"We're going to start on the old McAllister place on Albon road," said Jack.

"Decent." Boomer's broad smile filled the kitchen.

Jack Brennan started Brennan's Construction when he got out of high school. For his graduation present, he talked his parents into giving him the down payment for an old farmhouse that was in foreclosure. He spent the next six months rebuilding it. He then sold the farmhouse at a profit. His business took off from there. The house they now lived in was the third farmhouse he rebuilt. Both he and Eileen worked on the house during their engagement, and although they could have sold it at a nice profit, it became a wedding gift to each other. Neither could part with it.

The boys worked with their father during the summer and on Saturdays during the school year. Before he would take on a new project, Jack would always bring his sons out to the site. They would inspect the basement and if it didn't have one, they would go through the crawl space on their hands and knees. Jack's one rule that he hammered into his sons at every site was, "As long as the foundation is solid we can rebuild."

Boomer's eyes danced over the dilapidated farmhouse. "This is going to be so much fun, Little Bro." He could hardly contain himself. "Look at that roof. The whole thing has got to come off. Come on, let's check it out before Dad gets here."

Boomer unlocked the tool box built into the back of his truck. He tossed the hammer aside then easily lifted the sledge-hammer with one hand.

Cody followed Boomer up the front porch steps, giving his brother a wide berth. You never want to get to close to Boomer when he has a sledge-hammer. Cody learned early in life that Boomer likes to hit things. It didn't matter if it was a football player lined up across from him, or knocking down a non-supporting wall to enlarge a room. Boomer likes to hit, not to hurt, but to feel the titillating thrill of smashing something.

Cody followed Boomer through the doorway. Boomer tapped the sledge-hammer against the wall separating the front room from the kitchen searching for the studs.

"Wait!" Cody said.

"You know this wall's going to come down. People want open spaces today, not these dinky little rooms."

Cody shook his head. "Wait until Dad gets here."

Boomer twisted the sledge-hammer and paced like a lumbering elephant.

Cody tried to ignore his brother as he walked through the rooms. The oak floors were solid and probably worth more than the price of the house. There was some water damage near the windows, but that could be sanded out when they refinished the woodwork. Boomer was probably right, the one wall had to go so they could open up the living space. He thought they would take out the small front window and put in a picture window letting the light in. Cody could see the room taking shape. He ran his fingers over the molding, itching to get started not to tear down, but to rebuild.

Jack came into the house, his coffee mug in one hand and a thermos in the other.

Boomer pointed the sledge-hammer at the wall.

"That's coming down, right?"

Jack sipped coffee and nodded over the cup's brim.

Boomer grinned and smashed the sledge-hammer through the wall.

CHAPTER 3

In Grand Rapids spring was a season of tribulation. Fall, a season of celebration.

During the spring thaw, the village always kept one eye on the river. Some years, the cresting water would gently lap over the bank. When it receded it would leave behind a coat of silky mud.

But there were years when the river roared over its embankment and slammed into the shops along Main Street. Owners would mark their walls to show how high the river rose in a given year. When the water fell, the town always tried to make it like it used to be, and for that reason walking the streets of Grand Rapids was like taking a step back in time.

The Town Hall, O'Malley's Bar and Ludwig's Pharmacy were all etched in the historic registry looking the same as they did in the past century. The village became home to small antique and specialty shops. Children would eat ice cream in Promenade Park, while their parents sipped coffee on the veranda overlooking the river.

Fall would find artists trying to capture the sparkling beauty of leaves turning crimson, then gently drifting down to the water. During the Pumpkin Festival, the village blocked off Main Street and opened its arms to thousands of tourists from the city as if saying, "We haven't changed and we're still here."

Grand Rapids Photo Shop was on the river side of Main Street, down from Laura's Restaurant. On the first floor there was a small retail shop selling cameras and equipment along with a darkroom for photo development and a storage room. Above the shop was a two-bedroom apartment. The photo shop was the only home that Kim had ever known.

On Saturday morning before the shop opened, she sat at her computer monitor clicking through pictures that she took of last night's football game trying to decide which ones she would use in the next issue of the school's paper. She paused at the picture of Cody. He glanced up as the flash went off, his face a mask of abject disappointment. Kim knew she couldn't use it. The picture was too raw, too revealing. To use it would be like exposing Cody naked to the school. She clicked and copied the picture to her faces' folder then clicked back to the football game. There was the shot she could use, Cody caught just as he was releasing the ball as his brother leveled a Panthers linebacker. You could see the determination on Cody's face. His brother's back was to the camera, but every student would know it was Boomer.

"Are you up early, or haven't you gone to bed yet?"

Kim smiled at her grandfather.

"I slept for a couple of hours. I wanted to finish these shots for the paper before the shop opens."

"Let's see."

Kim nervously brushed her bangs from her forehead. Grandfather stood over her shoulder. She started at the beginning clicking through the photos she took of the game. She clicked through Cody's photo.

"Go back," said Grandfather.

Kim clicked the back button and held her breath. Grandfather leaned over her and studied the picture.

"You captured the moment. That picture tells the story without words. Use that one."

Kim shifted uncomfortably in the chair. Barely above a whisper, she said, "I can't."

"Why?"

She searched for words to explain her feelings to Grandfather. "It's just too...intimate." She looked at him and trying to justify her feelings she added, "Don't you think so?"

"No. Photographers take pictures. The intimacy comes from those who look at the pictures."

Kim blushed and glanced away.

"Grandmother's up in the kitchen. You should go eat before we open."

"I'm not hungry," replied Kim.

"Then go have some tea with your Grandmother. I'm afraid it's going to be a long day for you. I have to get to the university early. Some students are coming in before class to discuss their photo theses."

Reluctantly Kim closed the folders.

Upstairs, Grandmother balanced the tea cup and saucer in one hand. She set the tea before Kim, who nodded her thanks. Ahne, her grandmother, was Vietnamese. She did everything with one hand. Her other arm ended in a stump below the elbow. She was in her early 60's, her hair now more salt than pepper. She was small, barely five feet, with thin bones and delicate features.

Diluted Vietnamese blood flowed through Kim. Her grandfather was Polish, making her mother half-Vietnamese and half-Caucasian. Her father was Irish-German. Tourists who came into the shop would stare at her trying to figure out her nationality. A few were even so bold to ask outright, "What are you?" As a child she ignored the taunts of 'mutt' and 'mongrel' from boys on the schoolyard.

Sitting in the kitchen with her grandmother, Kim felt her Vietnamese heritage. Her grandmother was shy, reticent and hardly ever went out in public. In the evenings, when the shop closed, she would go down and clean and stock the shelves, but she wasn't comfortable being in the shop when there were customers. When she spoke, which wasn't often, her accent made English sound more lyrical.

Grandmother set a bowl of noodles in front of Kim, then got a bowl for herself. Kim wasn't hungry, but she knew, for her grandmother, eating together was a ritual meant to be shared. Kim stirred the steaming noodles, then gently blew on a spoonful of them.

Kim inherited her grandmother's brown eyes and gleaming black hair, which fell to her shoulders. At 5 foot 2 she was 2 inches taller than Ahne, but still short for an American. At 16, her thin tomboyish figure was finally adding some curves she so desperately wanted.

Ahne poured Kim another cup of tea, then walked across the kitchen to the shrine. Against the wall was a small wooden table that came up to her grandmother's waist. On the table was a picture of Kim's mother and father. Ahne lit a joss stick and set it in a cup before the picture, then said a prayer in Vietnamese.

CHAPTER 4

Cody tried to concentrate on the Mass, but his mind kept wandering. He drifted in and out of Father O'Brien's sermon. He was with his mother sitting in the same pew they sat in every Sunday morning. His eyes roamed as they always did over the interior of St Patrick's. He knew every nook and cranny of the 125-year-old church.

Boomer and his father would show up for the major feasts, Easter, Christmas and Mother's Day, but they had long since stopped attending on a weekly basis. On Sunday mornings, all Cody wanted to do was sleep in like Boomer, but what drove him out of bed was the thought of his mother sitting in the pew by herself. The only time she would miss Sunday Mass was when flooding from the spring thaw would close the bridge linking Grand Rapids to St. Patrick's across the river in Providence.

Father O'Brien had been Pastor at St. Patrick's for over five years. And after the first year, Cody realized, just like the seasons return every year, so did Father O'Brien's recycled sermons. But Cody didn't really blame Father O'Brien, who was well past retirement age, because his simple sermons - though repetitious - seemed to give comfort to his mother and the elderly congregation.

The sermon ended and Cody chanced a glance across the aisle. Kim was with her grandfather. He thought it must be some sort of special occasion because she hardly ever came to St. Patrick's. In a small town, all the kids knew each other. They went to the same schools, same ice cream parlors, and when they were kids swung on the same swings. He had seen Kim for years, but all of the sudden it was like he was seeing her for the first time. She didn't look or act like the other girls at school. She was quiet and shy and always with a camera. When other girls would fawn over him because he was the high school's quarterback, she seemed to regard him as just another student.

When the congregation stood, Kim was lost in the crowd. Cody leaned forward so he could see her. There was an aura of mystery around Kim. Standing next to her grandfather, she didn't look like she belonged with him. Her grandfather was a good six inches taller, stocky with pale skin, a thick white mustache, and blue eyes behind thick glasses. Kim was small, delicate, with a heart-shaped face and almond skin. If he had to describe her in one word it would be "exotic."

In grade school on one of the 'parents' days' Kim brought and introduced her grandfather, Stanley Lewinski, who talked about photography and showed some nature slides. Cody knew besides owning the photo shop, her grandfather also taught classes at Defiance University. He wondered about Kim's parents. He had never seen them and no one ever talked about her mother and father.

When time came in the Mass for the sign of peace, Cody said, "Peace be with you," then kissed his mother on her cheek. He shook hands with the parishioners in front and behind him giving the same greeting. He leaned across the aisle and shook hands with Mr. Lewinski. Kim was standing on the other side of her grandfather. With his hand still extended, Cody took a step into the aisle. Kim's hand was soft and warm, her smile more from her eyes than her lips.

Cody didn't really mind going to church with his mother, what he couldn't stand was waiting around after Mass ended. His mother had a need to talk with every parishioner gathered in the vestibule. Cody crammed his hands deep into his pockets and bounced from foot to foot as Eileen went from one person or couple to the next. Kim and her grandfather left as soon as Mass ended. He wasn't sure, but he thought she looked back to him from the doorway.

Finally, Cody could see the finish line as they made their way to Father O'Brien. The church doors were open, letting in an invigorating autumn breeze. Eileen had just taken the Pastor's hand when the horn started beeping. She shot Cody a look that said this can't be happening, no one would be beeping a horn on a Sunday morning in the church's parking lot. They both looked out the doors. From inside the red truck, Boomer waved his hand over the roof. Mortified, her cheeks flushed, Eileen turned back to the Pastor.

Cody bit his lip trying to keep the smile off his face. He nodded to Father O'Brien, then said, "I'll see you at home, Mom." Like on the football field, he ducked and weaved his way out into the sunshine.

CHAPTER 5

Smiling and waving at his neighbors, Boomer slowly maneu-
vered his red truck past the parishioners walking to their cars.
As soon as he pulled out onto Route 24, he jammed the accel-
erator to the floor. The truck fish-tailed, knocking Cody back
into the seat.

Boomer laughed and let go with a boisterous, "Whoa."
Dressed in brown-green camouflage fatigues with a matching
cap, he playfully smacked Cody's knee. "Your gear's in back."

Cody unsnapped his seat belt, then reached behind the seat
for his fatigues. He took off his shoes and threw them in back.
He slid down his dress pants and tossed them over his shoulder
quickly followed by his shirt.

Boomer shouted above the roar of air streaming through
open windows. "Today's the day, Little Bro. We are going to
waste those suckers!"

Boomer's rambunctious feelings were contagious. Slipping
on his fatigues, Cody felt like he was morphing into a warrior. He tapped his hands on the dash like he was beating on a
tom-tom.

Boomer braked and turned onto the dirt road. The truck's
tires spewed a rooster tail of dust into the air. He veered off
the road and across the field toward a group of teenage boys
clustered at the edge of the woods near a half-dozen parked cars

and trucks. Boomer gunned the truck and headed straight for them. The boys broke and ran for cover in the woods. Boomer laughed, slammed on the brakes and spun the wheel. The truck slid to a stop where the boys had been standing.

Boomer snatched his rifle from behind the seat. He pushed the door open, stood, pumped the gun in the air, then lowered the rifle and sprayed paintballs into the overhanging leaves.

The boys emerged from the woods wearing camouflage fatigues, some store bought, some handmade. The ones who knew Boomer best laughed. The others came slowly forward, looking at Boomer as though he was an out-of-control ogre to be avoided at all cost.

Cody took his boots from the back of the truck, then sat on the ground and laced them up.

Garrett, the black center of their football team, who was almost as big as Boomer, shouted, "Where've you been? We've been out here for an hour. We were beginning to think you weren't going to show."

Boomer refilled his rifle's hopper with paintballs. "You mean you were hoping we weren't going to show."

"Yeah, yeah. Let's get started."

Smirking at Garrett, Boomer said, "Flip for it or shoot for it?"

"Whatever."

Boomer leaned his rifle against the truck. "Cody, get the horn."

Boomer took the ESS profile goggles from his bag. Most of the boys wore helmets that covered their ears, eyes, nose, and mouth. Boomer could never find a helmet that comfortably fit his large head. For his 18th birthday, Cody went online and ordered the foliage green eye safety system goggles used by special ops soldiers. Boomer thought they were the coolest thing. When he first got them he even wore them when they were remodeling houses. He slipped the single lens goggles over his head covering his eyes, eyebrows and bridge of the nose, then added his cap. Unlike the helmets the goggles didn't cover his mouth. When Cody pointed this out, Boomer laughed and said, "I guess I'll just have to keep my big mouth shut."

Cody retrieved the small air horn from the bag. Boomer and Garrett backed away from each other. When they were about 30 yards apart, they stopped. They looked like two gunfighters from the old west, each with a rifle in one hand at their sides, the barrels pointing down to the ground, and their fingers on the triggers.

The other boys moved to the side forming a single line by Cody.

Cody looked at Garrett, who nodded his helmet. When he looked at Boomer, his brother spit to the side, then with a cocky grin bobbed his head. The horn's short sharp blast shrieked the air.

Garrett pressed the trigger too soon. Paintballs bursts onto the ground as he raised the rifle.

Boomer lifted his rifle. From the hip he fired one short burst. A red bloom suddenly blossomed by Garrett's groin. Garrett's hips flinched. He dropped his gun and tried to swipe the red watery paint from the front of his pants.

The boys howled. Cody laughed so hard his eyes watered. Each time the laughter died down, one boy would start again and they'd all join back in.

Boomer pointed his finger at Garrett and shouted, "Losers walk!"

CHAPTER 6

They played capture the flag. Garrett, the captain of the Green team, took the green flag. His team, with green armbands, set up at the visitor's command post in a small clearing a couple hundred yards into the woods. The red's command post was the base of the large oak tree right inside the tree line. The object was to retrieve the enemy's flag and bring it back to the command post. In the game it didn't matter where you were hit with a paintball - if you got hit you were out of the game and had to freeze where you were. The game ended when the horn sounded, signifying the enemy's flag was captured and taken to the command post.

The first half-dozen times they played, Boomer's team always lost. Garrett knew Boomer's nature was to charge right into battle. Garrett would set the ambush and wait. Finally, after being caught in a crossfire that made him look like someone dumped a can of red paint on him, Boomer turned to Cody and said, "Little Bro, what are we doing wrong?"

At the red command post, Cody squatted. Using a stick, he diagrammed his game plan in the dirt. He pointed to where he wanted Jake and Paul to stay and defend their flag. He'd send Boomer up the middle with Nick and himself covering Boomer's flank. He glanced around for Chad, then looked back. Quiet and motionless, Chad was standing five feet away from him, his camouflage blending into the forest. His black-green, pointed, elongated helmet made Cody think of the Predator movies. He smiled and motioned for Chad to come to him.

Cody was on Boomer's right flank crouched behind an over-turned tree stump. Boomer was 10 yards ahead behind the base of a towering maple tree. Boomer kept glancing back at Cody and hand motioning, "come on let's go." Cody shook his head and tapped his wristwatch. He wasn't worried about Garrett attacking. From past games, he knew Garrett's plan was to the dig-in and wait. He knew he had to give Chad at least 10 more minutes. Sitting still, his helmet was stifling. He shifted his back to the tree stump, then lifted the helmet off his face and let it rest on top of his head. The forest air felt cool on his damp skin. He looked up at the forest canopy, mesmerized by the flaming reds, browns and oranges of rustling fall leaves. In some ways he wished they weren't playing a game and that he could just spend the afternoon leaning against the tree.

A stick thumped against the stump. Cody snapped his helmet down and quickly twisted forward. Boomer was frantically waving his hands and mouthing, "Let's go!" Cody checked his watch then lifted his hand. When Nick on the other flank lifted his, Cody pointed forward.

Some big men could be light on their feet. Not Boomer. Even though he was trying to be stealthy, he looked like a lumbering grizzly bear thrashing through the brush and fallen leaves. Cody darted from tree to tree, his eyes and rifle sweeping the entire field in front of him. Suddenly, Boomer charged forward, spraying the forest with red starbursts. He screamed a curse as paintballs smacked against him.

Cody dropped and rolled. From the ground he fired a burst into the brush, then scampered behind a tree. Nick shot from the other flank. All Cody could hear was his quick breaths in his helmet.

Frustrated and dejected, Boomer sat back on his haunches, cradling his rifle. One of the opposing team ran from one tree to the next. Cody sighted on the tree willing his heart rate and breathing to slow. As the enemy peered around the tree, Cody fired.

Red blooms burst on the tree and soldier as he screamed, "I'm hit!" The green team member came out from behind the tree, his fatigues splotched red. He lowered his rifle, then sank to a sitting position.

Cody refilled his hopper. He checked on his brother. Boomer's mouth was a tight line, his eyes like lasers cutting to a spot behind him. Cody didn't look back, but rolled as paintballs popped the tree. Staying low, Cody scampered into the brush. He heard shots from Nick's flank then Nick screamed, "I'm hit!"

Cody crawled on his belly through the brush. He checked his watch. If Chad was able to sneak behind the green team's line, he should either be near their flag, or better yet had retrieved the flag when the enemy's attention was focused on him, Nick and Boomer. Cody thought, "I've got to make sure Chad gets back." He stood and fired a quick burst at the enemy's last position.

"There he is!" shouted Garrett.

Cody broke and ran with brush scraping his pants. He jumped a log, then slid down behind it. He saw movement to his left. He fired a burst. He raised his head to see if he hit someone and suddenly a red star bloomed on the lens right before his eyes.

Staying low Garrett loped through the woods to Cody. He hovered over him smiling and taunting. "Got ya."

Cody sat up and wiped the paint from his mask. He turned from Garrett to look back at his brother. Boomer looked like he was ready to snap Garrett in two. The horn from the red command post blasted.

Garrett said, "What the…"

It took Boomer a few seconds to realize what happened. His face lit up. He sprang to his feet and screamed, "We've got your flag, Sucker!"

Cody stood. Boomer charged through the woods and knocked Garrett aside. He grabbed Cody's shoulders and shaking him, he yelled, "We beat 'em Little Bro, we beat 'em!"

CHAPTER 7

"Now that's more like it," said Boomer. "Last year really sucked. Christmas just doesn't look right without the white stuff."

They parked the truck between other cars lined up on the side of the dark country road and walked up the long plowed driveway. The air was crisp, frigid. They exhaled puffs of white clouds while snow crunched under their shoes. Cody hugged his arms to his chest, shivering in the cold. Boomer, carrying the gift in one hand and wearing only a sweater, seemed impervious to the winter freeze.

The Andersons' house and yard could have been a Christmas card. Six inches of pristine, powdery snow had fallen the night before. Miniature red, green and white lights blinked from the roof and decked the evergreens.

Boomer paused. "Now that's the way Christmas is supposed to look."

The Andersons owned the largest farm in the area. Chad Anderson was Cody's friend and classmate. His older brother, Jason, was a senior on the football team and their younger sister, Shelby was a freshman. Between Christmas and New Year's the Andersons would host a party for their children and their friends. Boomer had been walking up the Andersons' driveway for the Christmas party for the last 12 years and Cody the last

10. It was a tradition both boys looked forward to almost as much as Christmas Eve at their house.

The party was in a metal pole barn converted to serve as a giant recreation room next to the house. Before heading to the party it was customary for guests to first stop at the house and say hello to Mr. and Mrs. Anderson.

Boomer stomped his shoes on the front stoop. The wooden inside door was open but the glass storm door was closed. He rang the doorbell, and not waiting for someone to open the door, walked right in.

"Boomer," said Mr. and Mrs. Anderson at the same time. They looked happy to see him. Teenagers might be intimidated by his size, but most adults who had known Boomer his whole life knew he was just an oversized kid.

"Merry Christmas." Boomer almost tossed the gift like a football to Mrs. Anderson, but caught himself and held out the package.

"What could this be?" Mrs. Anderson said. "Not one of your mom's famous fruit cakes?"

Boomer laughed and continued their yearly ritual. He shrugged and held his hands up by his face saying how would I know.

"Make sure you give your mom my thanks."

Feeling his duty done, Boomer backed right into Cody, who pushed him to the side.

"Merry Christmas, Mr. and Mrs. Anderson."

Mr. Anderson said, "Same to you, Cody."

Impatient to get going, Boomer opened the storm door letting in a blast of frigid air.

Mrs. Anderson waved the boys away. "Go, have a good time at the party."

As the boys stepped out onto the stoop, Mr. Anderson added, "Boomer, don't break anything."

They followed the shoveled path from the house to the pole barn. Walking inside, Cody was enveloped with warmth from the wood-burning stove.

Boomer stopped. One foot pointed to tables laden with platters of sliced beef, ham and turkey, chips, cakes and homemade pies, the other foot pointed to his friends who were playing video games on a large-screen TV across the room. The food won out. He made a beeline across the concrete floor. He grabbed two plates, then quickly filled one with sandwiches. He scooped a handful of cookies, a piece of cake and a slice of pie on the other. Balancing a plate in each hand, he walked to the video games. The couch and floor were packed with kids playing or waiting to play. All it took was one look from Boomer and suddenly there was an opening for him on the end of the couch.

Cody tossed his coat on top of a pile of coats by the door. He could feel his cheeks flush with the room's heat. He took in his surroundings in the large open room. Dominating one corner and filling the room with the scent of pine was a decorated Christmas tree, the star on top almost touching the high metal cross beam.

There were probably 50 teenagers and he knew them all. Boys vastly outnumbered the girls. The few girls that were in the rec room had come with dates. Cody knew the ratio of boys to girls would change later. Boys came to the party early not wanting to miss out on the food. Later in the evening, girls would arrive in groups and all at the same time.

Cody went over to check out the games. A new 50-inch widescreen TV was hanging on the wall. The boys were playing the latest Call of Duty game. The game was a great equalizer. Boys on the football team partnered with kids who didn't play any sports. As they played the screen was divided into four sections. Two boys on the floor and two on the couch had controllers to maneuver their soldier through a section. The object was for the four soldiers to move and fight as a team.

Boomer woofed down his sandwiches and was attacking the desserts. Through a mouthful of cake he said, "Brandon you're pathetic." He reached over Brandon's shoulder and snatched the controller. "Le' me show you how to play."

Cody knew Boomer had settled in for the night. His brother would only relinquish his controller to get more food or use the john. Cody didn't share Boomer's and some of the other players' fascination with war games. When Boomer first started playing the Call of Duty series, he tried everything he could to get his brother to partner with him, but Cody had no interest in sitting for hours playing a video game. Boomer got to the point where he quit asking Cody to play. Many nights when Cody was up in his bedroom doing homework, he would hear Boomer in the next room playing Call of Duty online with other gamers.

Watching the latest Call of Duty game, Cody couldn't believe how realistic the graphics had become. It was spooky the way the soldiers looked so lifelike.

The boys hooted and hollered as they went from one battle scene to the next. The more vivid the carnage, the louder they shouted. The volume was pitched so high it felt like explosions were actually shaking the concrete floor.

Boomer was so immersed in the action, Cody felt like his brother was slipping inside the game.

A fireball engulfed one of the soldiers. Boomer laughed and shouted, "Flame on!"

Cody thought he could hear the soldier scream inside the inferno. Suddenly, he felt fantasy had crossed into reality. Watching the flames consume the soldier, Cody's chest tightened, his throat constricted, he couldn't breathe. He turned and ran across the room then out into the cold.

CHAPTER 8

Spring break meant only one thing for Boomer and Cody: Walleyes. Between mid-March and April the olive and gold fish would run from Lake Erie into the Maumee River to spawn. Fishermen would come from all over the country to stand hip to hip in waders in the cold river water hoping to bag their daily limit of six fish. Most of the fishermen would converge where the river would flow into the lake. Very few fishermen would venture up to the turbulent water of Grand Rapids.

The name Walleye comes from the ability of the fish's eyes- like a cat's - to reflect light. This gives Walleyes the ability to feed in waters with low illumination and turbid conditions, waters found downriver from Grand Rapids. Through the years, the boys had found their favorite spots far from the groups of anglers who were closer to the mouth of the Maumee.

The state set the minimum size of 15 inches for a keeper, but anything that small Boomer and Cody would toss back. They figured if it wasn't at least a 20 incher it wasn't worth cleaning. The boys fished for fun, but also to eat. You would get no argument from Boomer when fishermen said Walleyes are without a doubt the best-tasting freshwater fish in the world.

It was perfect fishing weather for Walleyes, cloudy with the temperature in the 50's and a 10-mile-an-hour breeze putting a nice chop on top of the water. Boomer was halfway between the riverbank and the island with swirling brown water up to the hips of his waders. His feet were as solid as a bridge column. Cody was also wearing waders, but casting from the riverbank. Even though the waders were made out of neoprene, after a half hour in the icy water his legs would start shaking and his teeth chattering.

Boomer was casting upstream using a leadhead jig. Cody, casting from the bank, was using a floating jighead. For the last couple of years, the boys had been fiercely debating the advantage of one jig over the other, with neither yielding any ground.

Boomer yanked the rod to set the hook in the fish's mouth. "Whoa!" The rod bent over the water as he tried to reel in. He shouted excitedly, "I got a monster out here!"

"You probably just snagged a turtle," said Cody.

"No! I can feel him. I don't know what it is, but it ain't no turtle. Come out and help me!"

Cody shivered thinking about going back into the cold river. He reluctantly reeled his line in, then set his rod on the bank.

The end of Boomer's rod looked and sounded like a bumble bee buzzing erratically.

"Hurry, Little Bro."

A few steps from the riverbank, the frigid water was up to Cody's hips. He fought the current trying to sweep him downstream. Boomer's face was a mask of concentration trying to bring the fish in without snapping the line or having the fish throw the hook. Cody slipped on a rock. He quickly pounced back up but now his jacket and hands were wet and icy water had slipped into his waders.

Boomer screamed, "It's a Walleye! Look at the size of that sucker!"

Cody fought his way through the current. He could see a large fish thrashing in front of Boomer.

Boomer tried to steady the line. "Get him!"

Cody inched forward trying to find some purchase for his feet on the slippery river's bottom. He quickly thrust his hands into the river trying to grab and squeeze the fish like he would a slick football. He tightened his grip to keep the fish scales from ripping his hands and pulled the jerking fish from the water and cradled it against his chest.

Boomer shifted his rod to his left hand. His large right hand grabbed the back of Cody's jacket. "Don't lose him!" He half-pushed, half-carried Cody to the riverbank. Cody stumbled up the embankment then tossed the Walleye to the ground. Boomer pressed the flopping fish down with one hand the other reached into his pocket and took out his pliers. He grabbed and twisted the hook as razor sharp teeth bit against metal. Cody kneeled back on his heels and stared in awe at the gasping fish.

Boomer said with boyish glee, "He's got to be four feet."

"She." Cody held his arm over the Walleye. "She's not four feet, but she's at least three."

"Wait until Dad sees her. I bet'cha she's been growing in the river for a hundred years."

Cody shook his head. "Decades maybe, not a hundred years, Walleyes aren't like turtles."

"Jees, she's a beauty," said Boomer, not quite believing he had really caught the fish.

Cody nodded. She was the largest, most beautiful Walleye he'd ever seen.

Boomer playfully ruffled Cody's hair. "I couldn't have landed her without you, Little Bro."

Cody glanced from the Walleye to Boomer. The smile came from inside and slowly spread to his face.

CHAPTER 9

Cody wondered why good times like spring break always go by so fast. He stood in front of his closet doing his nightly pre-school ritual, picking out what clothes he would wear in the morning.

Clutching a sheet of paper, Boomer barged into Cody's bedroom. "You've got to help me, Little Bro."

Cody knew what was coming. "Aw, Boomer. Not again."

Boomer gave a sheepish grin. He handed Cody the paper then collapsed on the bed.

Cody scanned the assignment sheet. "You had all spring break to do this. This is going to take hours."

Boomer waved it off like it was no big deal. "We'll have it done in no time."

Getting angry, Cody said, "Yeah! Right! *We'll* have it done in no time."

Looking crestfallen, Boomer stared at his feet.

Cody took a deep breath and exhaled. There were times like now when Boomer really ticked him off and all he wanted to do was tell him off, but when he looked at his brother, he swallowed the words. Boomer was Boomer. He was never going to change. Whatever his faults, he didn't think there was a better brother in the world. He sighed and said as his shoulders dropped, "We better get started."

Cody walked over and sat at his computer. He looked upon the research paper as a personal challenge, a sophomore writing a senior paper. He knew he'd easily be able to gather the information he needed off the Internet. Within minutes, he was completely absorbed in the project. He didn't know Boomer left, until he heard him playing Call of Duty in his bedroom. Cody couldn't understand why some kids would spend hours playing computer games when they could use that time to tap into the Internet. Sometimes he was completely overwhelmed by the knowledge at his fingertips. Hours quickly passed and the rough draft was done. Now came the hardest part, and the true challenge he faced: how to rework the paper so that Boomer's teacher would think he wrote it.

Cody took the sheets from the printer and carried them to Boomer's bedroom. He paused in the doorway. The only light in the room came from the computer's monitor. Boomer's face was silhouetted by battle scenes. Cody flipped on the overhead light.

"Hey!" The quick flash of annoyance disappeared as Boomer's eyes darted from the screen and found Cody. "Done already?"

Cody held out the paper. "You need to read this."

Boomer turned back to the monitor checking the action.

"Now, Boomer. I want to go to bed."

Boomer huffed. His blunt fingers pressed the keys to freeze the battle screen. He took the paper. His lips formed the words as he slowly read.

Finished, Boomer nodded and with a smug smile said, "This is really good."

"What are you going to do when you go off to college?" Cody said, "I'm not going to be there to help you."

Boomer pretended to study the term paper.

Cody waited.

Finally, Boomer said in a low voice, "I'm not going to college"

Surprised, Cody said much louder than he intended, "What?"

Boomer quickly got up and closed his bedroom door then sat back down. "I hate school. You know how much I hate it. No way am I going to spend four more years in school."

"But...what about your football scholarship?"

"They can't make me take it."

"So...what are you going to do? Work with Dad?"

"I'm going in the army." Looking cocky and determined Boomer said, "I've already talked to the recruiter."

Cody felt like the room was starting to spin. He eased down on the edge of Boomer's bed. He looked from Call of Duty on the computer to Boomer. He felt like someone tackled him and the football jammed his gut. When he thought about the future, Cody pictured Boomer going off to college, playing football. He'd go up and watch his games. Maybe sometimes hang with him in the dorms. Boomer would come home for the holidays, Thanksgiving, Christmas and spring break when the Walleyes run. They'd be apart but still together. Now suddenly, all that changed, and it scared him.

Trying to keep his rising anxiety from his voice he said, "It's not like playing a game."

Boomer's hand waved Cody's words away.

"Iraq. Afghanistan. Soldiers die over there."

"I know that."

"I don't think you do. It's not like playing paintball in the woods. You get shot over there you don't get up and walk away."

"I'm not going to get shot." Boomer tapped his chest. "I'm the one who's going to be doing the shooting."

Cody's lips squeezed into a tight line.

"Besides, they got all this body armor you wear over there. Bullets bounce right off you."

Trying to get Boomer to change his mind, Cody said, "If you don't want to go to college stay here ... work with Dad."

Boomer emphatically shook his head. "No!"

The two brothers stared at each other.

Cody was frustrated, perplexed. Why was Boomer changing their future? He threw his hands up and asked, "Why?"

"Why what?"

"Why are you doing this? You're changing everything. Why all of the sudden do you want to be a soldier?"

Boomer was surprised with the way Cody was acting. He had expected Cody's congratulations and that his brother would be as excited as he was. He took it for granted that Cody understood why he wanted to be a soldier. "Remember the first time I took you out to Buffalo Rock."

Cody motioned to go on.

"I pulled you up on the boulder and we stood looking up and down the river. I told you how Ottawa Indian warriors used to stand in the very same spot guarding their village."

Cody said, "I remember."

Boomer struggled searching for words that would convey what he wanted to say. "Every time ... I climb up on Buffalo Rock ... I feel like I'm one of those warriors." Watching Cody's face, Boomer said, "You don't understand."

"Go on."

"I want to be a warrior."

CHAPTER 10

Kim was so frustrated she wanted to cry. She had 150 seniors dressed in their caps and gowns sitting on the bleachers in the gym. It felt like it was 100 degrees and she was starting to perspire like everyone else. No matter where she stood, she just couldn't get the right angle to capture all the students.

The seniors were past the point of snapping out quick barbs, which she tried to ignore, or taunting her, which was even worse. Now everyone was silently glaring at her just wanting to get the picture over and done with.

She knew what the problem was, she wasn't tall enough to get the angle she needed. In desperation she looked around the gym. She held up a finger and shouted, "Just give me one minute."

Completely out of character, she raced across the gym, kicked off her shoes, and in a graceful leap jumped up on the balance beam. She pirouetted on one foot and faced the students. As she spread her bare feet for balance, she quickly raised the camera and snapped the picture. She smiled as she captured the look of surprise on the students' faces - a look she knew must be reflected on her own face. It was a fun shot, but not one she could use in the yearbook.

She lowered the camera and surveyed the students from her perch on the beam. She felt the inner tug of satisfaction that came from knowing she finally found 'the spot.' She brought the camera up and focused. She lifted her hand and shouted, "This one's for your kids." As the seniors smiled, she snapped the picture.

The graduation ceremony was held on the football field. A raised platform was erected by the 50-yard line. The seniors were arrayed in folding chairs in front of the platform. Parents, friends, and family members were seated in the bleachers under a sparkling blue sky. Kim was on the platform just off to the side. As each senior came up to receive their diploma she would take their picture. The principal asked the students and families to hold any cheers or applause until the end of the ceremony, but that didn't stop a number of students from shouting, "Boomer! Boomer! Boomer!" as he crossed the stage. If he was embarrassed, he sure didn't show it. He towered over the diminutive principal with a smile almost as wide as his pumpkin-like face. He held the diploma up and waved it like a flag at his family in the bleachers. Cody stood and pumped his fist in the air. The students broke out in spontaneous applause.

When the ceremony was finished, Kim wandered among students and family groups lingering on the football field. It was a beautiful spring day, the air crisp and clear after an early morning shower, the field a lush emerald. A number of seniors seemed reluctant to leave their high school days. Cody's mother was taking a picture of her two sons and her husband.

Kim waited then said, "Let me take a picture of the four of you, Mrs. Brennan."

"Could you?" said Mrs. Brennan.

"Sure." Kim took the camera from Eileen. The husband and wife stood together with the boys like bookends. Kim lifted the camera then shook her head, the background was all wrong.

A picture needs to tell a story. She moved and repositioned the Brennan family so that the school was now the background.

She lifted the camera and brought their faces into focus, Boomer with his habitual wide smile next to Mr. Brennan who was beaming like a proud father. Mrs. Brennan's smile seemed forced. Her eyes betrayed her. Kim felt an undertow of sadness coming from Eileen. In the afternoon light, Cody's blue eyes dominated his face. He didn't have his brother's happy-go-lucky smile. Cody always seemed somewhat serious even when he smiled. She took the picture then moved in and handed the camera back to Eileen.

Kim lifted her camera that was hanging from a strap around her neck. "Let me take a picture of the two boys."

Boomer swung his arm around Cody's neck and pulled his brother's head to his chest. As Cody's struggled to pull free, Boomer said, "Hurry up. Shoot."

Kim snapped a picture. Boomer laughed and let his brother go. Cody stood looking warily at Boomer who motioned him forward and said, "Come on Little Bro." Cody stood by Boomer's side. Boomer wrapped his huge arm around Cody's shoulder.

Kim focused the picture. Hidden behind the camera she could stare at Cody to her heart's content.

CHAPTER 11

Cody couldn't sleep. He tossed his blanket off because he was too hot, then pulled it back on because he was too cold. It seemed like his bedside clock was frozen in time. He wanted to fall asleep, but he was afraid. When he woke up it would be tomorrow and he did not want tomorrow to come.

It was eerily quiet as if the house knew what changes the morning would bring. Boomer was leaving and Cody was scared. He could not picture his life without his big brother. How could a day start without Boomer wolfing cereal at the breakfast table and babbling on about the day's adventures that lay ahead?

Cody wanted to go to Boomer's bedroom and beg him to stay. He knew he was being childish and selfish. He knew why Boomer wanted to be a soldier. He wanted to support him, but every time he thought of life without Boomer his stomach tightened so much it felt like his intestines would burst.

Time passed and moonlight skirted the floor. Through the open window wind skated across the screen and he heard soft sobbing. He knew his mother was sitting on the swing on the porch below his window. For weeks she argued, then pleaded, first with Boomer and then with her husband, but Boomer's mind was made up and Jack supported his decision.

Cody rolled on his side and curled his knees up by his chest.

Cody awoke to the smell of sizzling bacon. He was disorientated for a few seconds, then sprang out of bed and raced to Boomer's bedroom. The room was empty. He ran to the top of the steps and stopped, then breathed when he heard Boomer's voice in the kitchen. He went to the bathroom and got ready to start the day.

In the kitchen, Boomer looked like he was living out one of his favorite dreams. On the table before him were cinnamon rolls smothered with white icing, egg soufflé with sausage, home-made hash browns, pancakes dripping butter and syrup, crisp bacon, a pitcher of milk and another of orange juice.

When Cody walked into the room, the laugh lines around Boomer's eyes were in full force, his mouth too full to talk. Cody took his seat. Eileen brought another plate of pancakes to the table. Boomer quickly speared a couple and snatched them back to his plate.

Cody knew his mother never went to bed. She still had on the same clothes she wore yesterday. Her hair was disheveled, her eyes puffy. She seemed tired and fragile and suddenly old with an air of resignation. She went to the oven and took out a baking sheet of chocolate chip cookies and set them on the counter next to the oatmeal raisin cookies she baked earlier.

Cody forked some pancakes onto his plate. He wanted to ask his mother if she was OK, but instead asked, "Where's Dad?"

Eileen used the spatula to lift cookies off the sheet. "He already had his breakfast. He's out checking the SUV."

Boomer grabbed a cinnamon roll and used it to soak up the remaining syrup from his plate. In two quick bites the roll disappeared in his cavernous mouth. He released a great contented sigh. He pushed back from the table and jiggled his stomach.

"I think, I am finally full."

Boomer dropped his duffle bag on the porch. "Come on Little Bro."

Cody followed him to the driveway. Boomer slowly walked around his truck, his eyes caressing every line. He wiped a smug of dirt off with his sleeve then stood with a look of pride and longing. He reached into his front pocket, pulled out the keys and thrust them at Cody.

"Here."

Cody said, "What?"

"I want you to drive her while I'm gone."

"No way! We'll put her in the garage until you get back."

"You know, for being so smart, you've got a lot to learn about trucks. Trucks don't squat in garages. Check the oil and keep her clean."

"But..."

Boomer tossed the keys.

Cody caught them. He knew when his brother made up his mind there was no arguing with him. His eyes nodded his acceptance.

That taken care of, Boomer said, "Time to hit the road."

Eileen set the sack packed with cookies next to Boomer's duffle bag. She knew it would be too much for her to see Boomer off at the airport. She needed to say her goodbyes on her own porch. She tapped her inner strength. Her son would not see her cry.

As Boomer came up the steps, she opened her arms and said, "Come here." She held him with a sudden fierceness, then reluctantly let go. "You take care of yourself." She caressed his cheek. "I don't want you getting into any trouble."

Jack shouted from the SUV, "We've got to go!"

Eileen bent, picked up the sack and handed it to her son. She tried to put a smile in her voice. "Don't eat them all today."

Boomer leaned and kissed her cheek. "Luv ya, Ma."

Eileen squeezed her eyes and gently pushed him away.

Cody grabbed Boomer's duffle bag and carried it to the SUV. He tossed it in the back seat, then followed it in. Jack was behind the steering wheel. When Eileen looked at him, he couldn't hold her gaze. Boomer sat up front. When they got to the end of the long gravel driveway, Boomer didn't look back, only forward. Cody was the one who turned and waved to their mother.

CHAPTER 12

Sprinting across the football field, Cody was sucking wind. His thighs felt like they were on fire. He crossed the line and slowed to a fast walk with his hands clasped behind his head. His face was scarlet, sweat dripping into his eyes, his mouth gulping air like a fish out of water. He couldn't help smiling at his teammates who were going through the same painful contortions. And they hadn't even started two-a-days.

He was glad to be back on the football field and soon to be back in school. Summer was a bummer. The days were OK because he spent those working with his dad and his crew, but nights and weekends for the most part sucked. With Boomer gone the whole dynamics of summer changed. His big brother wasn't there for him to joke and horse around with. Fishing wasn't the same when he went by himself. Without Boomer's mischievous grin and booming laugh, the house seemed almost somber. Most of all it wasn't a summer of adventure. He had no tall tales to tell his teammates of the troubles Boomer got them into and how he managed to get them out.

If someone asked him to describe his summer in one word he would shout *boring*.

Being back among his teammates, Cody realized the runner-up word for the summer was *lonely*.

As his breath came back, Cody took stock. He was in shape - just not football shape. Over the summer he worked at least eight and sometimes as many as 12 hour days. While some of his teammates were in the weight room pumping iron, he was hoisting drywall and bags of cement. There were days he worked so hard that soon as he finished dinner he went straight to bed. Since last season he sprouted an inch and a half and added 15 pounds. He was no longer the lanky sophomore but a junior at 6 foot 2 and 195 pounds with the build of a linebacker. The biggest change was his throwing arm. The work crew and even his dad used pneumatic nail guns. They'd pull a trigger to drive a nail completely into wood or drywall. Not Cody. During the summer, he pounded thousands of nails with a 20-ounce high carbon steel claw hammer with a solid hickory handle. The motion of swinging a hammer was just like throwing a football especially the twist of the wrist at the end. Neither he nor his coach could believe the added zip he now put on his passes. The football shot like a dart into receivers' hands.

What he needed before the season started was to get his wind back, but he knew that part was easy. He dropped down into a three-point stance then sprinted across the field. All he had to do was run.

Walking with his teammates to the parking lot after practice every muscle in his body ached. But it felt good. He felt alive.

Jason Carpenter, who had taken Garrett's place at center, and who everyone called 'Carp' shouted, "Cody, couldn't you get any closer?"

Chad laughed and said, "Why don't you just leave Boomer's truck at home and walk to practice."

Gump added, "Cody, you want me to give you a ride out to your truck?"

Cody waved the friendly jeers away as he kept walking and left his teammates behind. Boomer's red truck was at the end of the parking lot. There wasn't another car or truck within 30 yards. Out of habit, Cody did a slow walk around the truck while saying a silent prayer that he wouldn't find any scratches or dents.

He climbed up into the truck's high seat. He sat for a second, as he always did, before he turned the ignition and thought about Boomer. He wondered where he was right now, what was he doing? He tried to get Boomer to email him, but Boomer wasn't a writer. When he first left, Boomer would call almost every day as he said, "Just checking in," but the calls were becoming less and less frequent. Cody knew Boomer was excited that his basic training was done and couldn't wait to find out where he would be stationed. He also told Cody that no matter what he'd find a way to stop home before he shipped out. He wanted to see his Little Bro kick some big time ass on the football field, hopefully against the Panthers.

He started the truck and drove out of the parking lot onto the two-lane country road. Tree limbs formed an arch over the road and sunlight played among the leaves. The few houses were set back from the road with long gravel or concrete drive-ways, and fat metal septic tanks looking like hippos in the yard.

Mr. Shonebarger was checking his mailbox on a wooden pole by the side of the road. He looked up, recognized the truck, and smiled, then waved. Cody was amazed at the number of people who knew Boomer's truck and thus Boomer. He expected the kids at school to recognize the truck because his brother was such a large presence in the rural high school. But wherever he went, grocery store, gas station, library, hardware store, everyone knew the truck and the first thing out of their mouths was, "How's Boomer?"

His standard reply, "He's OK." Their follow-up line was usually, "Make sure you tell him, I said hi."

Cody pulled into the driveway. His mother was watering plants. It seemed since Boomer left his mother was spending more and more time in her garden. He wondered what she was going to do when winter comes.

CHAPTER 13

Of all his classes, the one Cody looked forward to most was Honors English. Ever since he was a kid he loved to read. His favorite books were historical fiction. He admired writers who could transport him to a different time and place and make their stories come alive.

He took his seat in the classroom, got out his notebook, and when he looked up, she was sitting next to him. His stomach did one of those flutters like when he threw a long pass and watched it sail right into the receiver's hands.

Kim said, "Hi."

Cody said, "Hey." He tried to think of something else to add, but his mind went blank. Finally he blurted, "You're in this class."

Kim's eyes widened and she gave a slow nod.

Cody almost expected Kim to say, "Dah." He wanted to crawl under his seat for saying something so lame.

Kim asked, "How's Boomer."

Cody hid his embarrassment behind a laugh. "He's OK."

During class, Cody tried not to look at Kim, but he failed, miserably. When she would catch him staring, he'd quickly dart his eyes away, but soon they would return. It was like his eyes were magnetized to her face. He didn't understand, why? In the locker room the boys would go on and on about Tiffany's huge knockers, or Audrey's long legs and even Beth's so called perfect butt. Kim had none of those features, but yet there was just something about her.

Class ended and they both stood. Side by side they were such a mismatch; Cody a foot taller than Kim's 5 foot 2 inches, Cody with blonde hair and blue eyes, Kim raven black hair and coffee eye. Cody, built like a linebacker; Kim, like a petite gymnast.

Kim flashed a coy smile. "See you tomorrow."

Still tongue tied, Cody just bobbed his head.

Cody was still trying to figure out if he should ask Kim for a date. After Friday's class, Kim mentioned she was going to the Butterfly House to take pictures. Somehow, they decided they would go together on Sunday afternoon.

Cody angle-parked Boomer's truck in front of the Photo Shop. He did a quick check in the sun visor's mirror. He finger combed his hair, then said, "Ah gross," as he noticed the half moon perspiration stains under his arms. Cupping his hand in front of his face he breathed out then snatched a mint from the center console. He told himself to chill. He wasn't this nervous before a game.

The shop had one of those old-fashion bells that jingled from the top of the door when the door was opened. Kim's grandfather came out of the back room and stood behind the counter.

"Hi, Cody."

"Hello, Mr. Lewinski."

"What can I help you with today?"

"Ummm…" Cody glanced at the ceiling as he heard footsteps above his head. He followed the steps to the back wall then heard the quick pitter-patter of little feet on a stairway. Kim entered the room and Cody's face lit up.

Kim ducked behind the counter and picked up her camera and a yellow legal pad. Cody detected a smile beneath Mr. Lewinski's mustache. He realized Mr. Lewinski was playing with him, Kim's grandfather knew why he was here.

Kim said, "I'll be back later."

"Later?" said Stanley.

Kim rolled her eyes. "We're just going to the Butterfly House. Cody's helping me with the article for the Gazette."

"Oh."

Kim's thin lips curled up at the edges as she walked to Cody "I'm taking the pictures." She held out the legal pad. "And Cody's writing the story."

Cody almost fumbled the pad as she let it go. He wasn't sure what was going on as he followed Kim out the door.

Cody paused on the sidewalk. When he was with his mom he always opened the truck's door for her. The big question was, should he do the same for Kim?

He circled in front of her and said, "Let me get it." He opened the door.

Kim stared up at the high bucket seat. "Maybe I should get a running start."

Cody laughed. "There's a handle..." He moved closer and tried to point out the handle without touching Kim.

"Got it." She grabbed the handle and sprang like a lithe puma into the seat. She settled in and put on her black oval sunglasses.

Cody climbed into the truck and snapped on his seat belt. He looked back over his shoulder. Traffic was typical for a Sunday afternoon during late summer in Grand Rapids. Tourists from the city strolled from shop to shop on Main Street. He slowly, carefully backed out onto the street.

When he crossed the bridge to Providence, he said, "You were kidding, right?"

"About what?"

"Writing an article for the Gazette."

"No. We are doing a story for the paper."

"I've....never written an article."

"You be fine. Just remember the five W's."

"Five W's?"

"Basic journalism; who, what, where, when, and why. Answer the five W's and you've got your story."

Cody shook his head feeling like everything was just going too fast. He thought dodging blitzing linebackers was hard.

"Besides," Kim said, "the job comes with perks." She turned in the seat, took off her sunglass and smiled at Cody. She tapped the stem of the sunglasses by her lips.

Cody stole a glance at Kim then quickly looked back to the road. He swallowed his mouth suddenly dry. "Perks?"

"We get in for free."

Cody couldn't help laughing and Kim laughed with him.

CHAPTER 14

They drove down the two-lane blacktop road. The corn was so high Cody felt like he could stick his hand out the window and snatch a husk. Suddenly, there was a break in the cornfield. Cody flicked his turn signal and pulled into the gravel parking lot. He had never been inside the Butterfly House, but through the years he had explored the adjacent corn mazes. He and Boomer and their friends all agreed the mazes would be an ideal place for an epic paintball battle, but the owner said, "No way." In fall, especially around Halloween, the mazes were a local tourist attraction. The owner didn't want his fields trampled and splattered with paint.

The Butterfly House was a white, single story, square, aluminum building on a concrete slab. Cody grabbed the legal pad and a pen from the glove compartment. Before he even got out of the truck, Kim was taking photos. He leaned against the truck and studied her. She moved with a quick efficiency of motion. The camera seemed so natural in her hands it was almost like it was part of her.

He followed her inside. There was a large anteroom filled with everything imaginable about butterflies. Shelves and display cases were packed with butterfly books, tapes, toys, puzzles, maps, pens, stickers. Kim went right to work with the camera. Cody started jotting down notes on the legal pad.

Cody figured the woman walking toward him had to be the owner. She was elfin, middle-aged and covered with butterflies, but not real butterflies. Her blouse was imprinted with images of butterflies. Silver butterflies dangled from charm bracelets on both wrists. A royal blue butterfly painted on white porcelain hung from her neck. She had butterfly shoelaces and butterfly pins in her hair. Even her eyeglasses were shaped in the form of open butterfly wings.

Kim materialized at his side and said, "Hi Judy." She motioned Judy to stop, then took her picture.

The interview went much easier than Cody expected. Judy loved to talk - especially about butterflies. As she talked, her hands fluttered like butterfly wings. Cody struggled to keep up with Judy's rapid banter as he quickly filled pages.

There were two doors leading into the butterfly room. The first door opened to a closet-size chamber and needed to be closed before they opened the second door so that no butterflies would escape. When they walked through the second door, Cody felt like he stepped into a tropical forest, the air hot and humid with the rich moist smell of plants. Butterflies fluttered everywhere. Their colors were amazing: silver –spotted skippers, green swallowtails, zebra swallowtails, eastern tailed blues, spring azures, painted ladies, wood nymphs, red admirals, monarchs, blue mormons. Graceful. Delicate. Incredibly beautiful. Cody was afraid to move for fear he might crush one.

Kim gracefully eased among the butterflies with a wondrous smile. Their eyes met and it was like they both said, I know just how you feel.

Cody sat at the computer glancing from the legal pad to the words he typed on the monitor. He had the five W's, but that wasn't enough. He had facts but not feelings. He wanted readers to feel the wonder of opening the door to the butterfly room. He went back to the beginning and started again.

When he was finished, his finger hovered over the key to email the story to Kim. Self-doubts whispered in his mind. What if she doesn't like it? What if it isn't any good? He read the story again, but he knew it was done. Impulsively he hit the send key. He sat back and released a sigh of accomplishment mixed with anxiety.

CHAPTER 15

Flat on his back, Cody sucked in a gulp of air. His toes and his fingertips tingled. He had almost forgotten what it felt like to have a linebacker drive a helmet into his chest as he stepped forward to throw a pass. For a second he thought Boomer was standing over him.

"You OK, Cody?"

Cody's head cleared and he focused on the center, Carp. As his chest painfully expanded, Cody gritted his teeth. He rubbed his hand on his left side. The ribs hurt, but not with the sharp pain and accompanying feeling of nausea that he had before when they were broken. He rolled over onto his knees and pushed up from the ground. He stood, took a couple of breaths, then followed Carp to the huddle.

Carp shot him a look of, what are you doing here? "It's fourth down. We're punting."

Cody glanced at the down marker, then to the scoreboard clock. "Shit!" He angrily flashed a time-out to the ref then jogged to the sideline.

Coach Stutz grabbed Cody's helmet and asked while checking his quarterback's blue eyes, "Are you OK?"

"I'm good."

Coach Stutz released Cody's helmet and turned back to the field.

Cody looked up to the scoreboard. It definitely wasn't the way he envisioned their first game of the season. The Titans were beating them 34-10 in the fourth quarter. They fell behind early and in the third quarter gave up their running game. Now the Titans were blitzing on almost every play and Cody had to scramble for his life. He lifted and propped his helmet on top of his head, then squirted a stream of water into his mouth.

The Titans offensive line dominated the fourth quarter. They overpowered the smaller defense and in a time-consuming drive, ran the ball down the field for another touchdown.

With under two minutes left in the game, Cody knew there was no way they were going to mount a comeback. All he wanted to do was get a touchdown. If the Titans were going to blitz him every play, he was going to dink them with short passes over the middle. And that's what he did. A quick three-step-drop and bam - the ball was out of his hand. After five straight completions they were at the 50-yard line. Cody hit Chad on a quick slant. Chad ducked, then spun. The safety and the cornerback collided above him. Chad broke free and raced to the end zone. Cody ran after his receiver, pumping his fist in the air.

It was a pretty dejected locker room. After all of the grueling two-a-days and pre-season high expectations, the team got thoroughly pounded, 43-17, in their first game. If they kept playing like they did today it would be a long season. If Boomer were here he'd find a way to get something positive out of the loss, get their heads back up.

Last year they had a running game because Boomer and Garrett could blow a hole in any line. The running game opened up their passing game. Looking at his teammates, Cody realized there wasn't anyone who even came close to Boomer's

CHAPTER 16

They ate dinner in Laura's Restaurant. Cody was ravenous. He devoured two double cheeseburgers, an order of fries, one of onion rings and a large chocolate shake. Kim shook her head in wonder. She could barely finish her oriental chicken salad. They sat at a table for two by the front door. Kim would glance up every time the door opened just to see the looks on the faces. Students from the high school would recognize Cody, then look at Kim, then quickly do a double take back to both of them. Their surprised faces brought a smile to Kim's face. The adults in the restaurant all knew Kim from town, and if they were surprised to see her with Cody they managed to hide it much better than the teenagers.

They finished dinner, then walked out into the late summer evening air. Moths fluttered around the tops of the lampposts. Boomer's truck was parked in front of the restaurant, but the Photo Shop was just down the street.

Cody said, "I'll walk you home."

Kim started to say, "You don't have to," but swallowed the words.

They walked slowly, neither in a hurry, and not sure what to do with their hands.

The lights were on in the Photo Shop.

Kim said, "Come on. I want you to meet my grandmother." She used her key to open the door.

Startled, Ahne dropped the broom.

Kim quickly said, "It's just me, Grandmother."

Ahne relaxed then turned slightly away concealing her arm. She bent to pick up the broom.

Kim said, "This is Cody."

As Ahne stood, Cody stepped forward. He stopped, stunned. He stared at the diminutive Vietnamese woman.

Grandmother said, "Hello."

It took Cody a few seconds before he could say, "Hello."

Her voice soft, lilting, Ahne said, "I'll make some tea."

Confused and not sure what Ahne said, Cody turned to Kim who motioned him to follow her grandmother.

Upstairs, Cody sat across from Kim. He didn't notice Ahne's missing forearm until she set the tea before him. He tried to not look and to look at the same time. He shifted his focus to the small teacup. He never had tea before. He turned to Kim to follow her lead. Kim lifted her teacup then gently blew across the top. She took a dainty sip then set the teacup down.

When Cody mimicked her movements, Kim laughed, Grandmother smiled, and Cody started to relax.

Kim asked, "Did Grandfather go to bed?"

Ahne nodded then walked to the staircase. "I need to finish downstairs." She waited.

Kim caught her grandmother's silent message that she didn't want to leave them alone for too long.

"We'll just finish our tea," Kim said. "And then we'll be right down."

After Ahne went downstairs Cody said, "I didn't know your grandmother was ...Chinese?"

"Vietnamese."

"But you're not..."

Kim stood and walked to the small shrine and lifted the photo then brought it back to the table.

"My mother and father." She set the photo before Cody. "My mother was half -Polish and half-Vietnamese. I think my father was Irish-German."

Cody looked from the photo to Kim wanting to ask questions, but not knowing if he should.

Kim read his face. "My mother died giving birth to me. My father died in a car accident a few weeks later."

Cody didn't know what to say. "I'm ...sorry."

"I never knew them. All I have are photos."

"Your mother was beautiful."

With a fleeting glimpse of sadness and yearning Kim whispered, "Grandmother said, 'My father died of a broken heart.'" She carried the photo back to the shrine.

When she turned back to Cody it was like she returned to the Kim he knew. Her face eased into a smile and her whole body radiated gaiety.

"Grandmother and Grandfather raised me and if I don't get you downstairs right now, I'm going to be in big trouble."

Cody got into the truck and backed out into the street. Home was south, but instead he went north so that he could drive by the Photo Shop. Kim was standing in the doorway, just as he had left her, as if she knew he would drive by. He let the truck creep along with his arm hanging out the window. Kim extended her hand. The sidewalk separated them, but it was like they touched. Cody accelerated and drove the long way home.

CHAPTER 17

Cody parked in the empty area at the back of the short-term parking lot at Express Airport. He jumped out and did a slow walk around. He had spent the morning washing and polishing Boomer's truck until the fire-engine red finish sparkled in the sunlight. He clicked the remote entry, snapping the locks down. He started walking fast, sometimes almost skipping, to the terminal.

Inside the airport he paced with his hands in his pockets while continuously checking the flight monitor. His heart felt like it was going 100 beats a minute - but they were good beats. When the overhead board flashed that Flight 197 landed, he raced to the front of the waiting room.

Boomer was in the middle of the arriving passengers but he towered over them. When the brothers' eyes met identical smiles broadened their faces. Boomer, wearing his dark green dress uniform and beret, fought his way through the crowd. Cody raised his hands sure that Boomer was going to try and put him in a headlock. Boomer didn't go for the headlock, but the bear hug. He lifted Cody and spun him in circles. Spinning, Cody saw passengers smiling and kids staring in awe.

Cody went to grab Boomer's duffle bag off the luggage carousel, but Boomer pushed him aside. "Save the arm for the big game." Boomer easily hoisted the duffel onto his shoulder.

They walked together through the terminal to the parking lot. Everyone seemed to be staring at them. Boomer, the embodiment of today's soldier, could have stepped out of a recruitment poster. He nodded and smiled as he sauntered forward with a swagger in his step. Cody basked in his brother's limelight.

When they neared the short-term parking lot, Boomer looked like he was seeing a long-lost friend. He tossed his duffle bag into the truck's bed. Cody threw him the keys then walked to the passenger door. Boomer climbed into the truck. He turned the key in the ignition then sat with his eyes closed listening to the purr of the engine. Satisfied, he dropped the truck in gear and drove from the lot.

There wasn't a moment of silence during the ride from the airport to home. It was like they picked up were they left off yesterday not four months ago. Cody wanted to know all about basic training. Boomer told some stories that had Cody rocking with laughter. He knew his brother had to be exaggerating, but then remembering some of their escapades, he thought maybe they were true.

Cody asked Boomer where he was going to be stationed. Boomer waved the question away and instead asked about the team and the upcoming game with the Panthers.

When they pulled into the long gravel driveway, Jack was already on the porch. The screen door opened and Eileen came out wiping her hands on her apron.

Boomer parked and shut off the engine. He glanced from his parents on the front porch to his brother, his face glowing like it was Christmas morning or the start of the Walleye run.

Boomer popped opened the door. In a few quick strides he was on the porch. Letting his brother have his own moment, Cody sat and watched from the truck. Boomer gently hugged their mother then released her. He faced their father standing tall and strong in his crisp uniform. Boomer captured what they strived and competed for, the look of pride on their father's face.

CHAPTER 18

Friday night football. The stadium lights cast players' shadows on the field. Bleachers were brimming with the Panthers red and gold jackets on one side and the Generals blue and white on the other. The cool autumn evening air was filled with the cacophony of competing marching bands.

Coach Stutz made Boomer an honorary team captain for the game. Dressed in his army uniform, he went from player to player pounding backs, shaking shoulder pads and twisting face mask, getting the team psyched, working them into a frenzy. Prowling the sideline, he was more intimidating than any drill sergeant.

Cody tossed light warm-up passes with Chad, trying to vanquish the pre-game jitters. It was a perfect night for passing, no wind, a clear sky and a dry field. As his arm loosened, he put zip into his dinks.

They were playing in the Panthers stadium. The announcer called the captains' names for the coin toss. When Boomer's name was called a chant went up from Generals bleachers, "Boomer, Boomer, Boomer." As they walked to midfield, Cody was surprised when some of the fans in the Panthers bleachers shouted, "Boomer," and saluted.

Boomer stood at attention as they played the National Anthem. Cody had heard the song hundreds of times, but tonight, standing next to his brother, the words suddenly had meaning.

The Generals took the opening kickoff out to their own 30-yard line. Cody quickly huddled the team then set them in the spread offense. He was the only one in the backfield - everyone else was on the line. On the opening drive he was 12 for 12 hitting five different receivers and covering 70 yards for their first touchdown. Dink. As they ran back to the side-line fans were hooting and stomping their feet. Boomer ran onto the field and high-fived his brother and the rest of the offense.

The Panthers answered with their power running game. They didn't put the ball in the air. They didn't have to. The fullback and tailback were grinding out seven yards a carry and eating up the clock. Rubbing it into the Generals' faces, they didn't even try to kick the extra point, but lined up and easily ran the ball in for two points.

Cody was in the zone. It was like he had laser sights. Where ever he looked, that's where the ball went. The Panthers' pass rush was a non-factor because he got rid of the ball so quickly. On their second drive he was 10 of 11 covering 63 yards for the second touchdown and a quick slant to Chad for the two-point conversion.

At the half the Generals were up 31-24. Cody didn't want to go to the locker room. He didn't need a break. He felt good. His uniform looked like he just put it on. If he kept playing the way he was playing he would easily break the school records for completions and passing yards.

The Generals defense was another story. Their uniforms were grass and dirt stained, some bloody. Two of the first string-ers were out with injuries, Gradkowski with a broken finger, and Sweeney with a sprained ankle.

Boomer did what he always did. He got in each player's face and when he was finished that player knew in the second half he would play his best game.

The Panthers took the second half kick-off and eight plays later scored their fourth touchdown and fourth two-point conversion.

When the Generals got the ball back, the Panthers made their half-time adjustments. They gave up trying to blitz Cody. Instead, they concentrated on jamming the receivers before they got off the line to disrupt Cody's rhythm. They had the linemen get their hands up to try to knock down his passes and also shift along the line to take away his passing lanes. And it worked.

Cody's first pass was knocked down. His second was too high because he had to zip it over a linebacker. The third pass was incomplete when his receiver slipped while making his cut. Cody had already zipped the ball to where the receiver should have been.

Cody looked to the sideline to see if Coach Stutz was going to send in the punting unit. The Coach called a time-out. Cody knew what the Coach was thinking; the defense hadn't been able to stop the Panthers running game all night. The only way the Generals could win was by trading touchdowns. They couldn't punt the ball away.

Coach Stutz told Cody to dance and sent him back onto the field. Not scramble, but dance. Drop back, stay in the pocket but shift just enough to get the passing lanes back. On fourth and 10, Cody danced. Soon as he saw Chad, he hammered the ball to him. Somehow Chad managed to hang on to the bullet. He jogged back to the huddle while rubbing his chest. Five plays later the Generals took back the lead.

The fourth quarter was a chess match. Both coaches knew whoever scored last would win the game. The good news was the Generals surged ahead 47-40, the bad news was there was still five minutes left in the game. The Panthers began their methodical march down the field burning up the clock, but nobody told the Panthers tailback that he was supposed to limit himself to five to eight yards a carry. He broke loose at the 45 and raced 55 yards for the go-ahead touchdown. There was still three minutes left in the game.

Boomer came over to Cody and said "Little Bro." He smiled. The rest was said with their eyes. They both knew it was Cody's time. Cody didn't want to go out on the field, he wanted to save that moment with his brother.

Cody danced and dinked. It was absolutely exhilarating. With each completion the fans roared. Cody couldn't miss and he knew it. When Chad caught Cody's dart in the end zone it was pandemonium. The only thing that kept the Generals fans in the bleachers was the 30 seconds left on the clock. Cody ran over to his brother feeling like his feet weren't touching the ground.

The brothers stood together. Everyone in the stadium held their breath as the ball took flight. The Panthers tailback caught the kickoff at the 15. He faked left then spun right. He broke a tackle at the 20 and another at the 25 and then he was in the open.

Boomer screamed, "No!" He charged out onto the field.

It took Cody a split second to realize that Boomer was going to tackle the Panthers tailback. Boomer was bigger and stronger, but Cody was faster. Cody tackled Boomer from behind. The tailback jumped over Boomer and raced to the end zone.

Boomer sat up looking bewildered like he didn't know where he was. He shook his head as if shaking off a dream.

The referee in the end zone raised his hands for the touchdown. The Panthers fans swarmed onto the field.

The two brothers sat in the middle of the Panthers football field. His army uniform stained and crumpled, Boomer had a sheepish look on his face. Cody looked at the Generals fans staring at them. He realized how absurd they must look. He couldn't help it, he laughed, and then Boomer started laughing. Cody knew he would be hearing this 'Boomer story' for his lifetime.

CHAPTER 19

Cody tried to imagine what it would have been like to live in the Ottawa Indians' village. He stood on the bluff just like Indians did centuries ago, looking down at the large limestone formation in the river. To the Indians, the formation looked like a buffalo charging upstream through the rapids and that's why they called it Buffalo Rock.

Boomer was pursuing one of his favorite hobbies: searching for arrowheads. He was at the edge of the clearing near the woods in an area called Fallen Timbers. Ages ago, a tornado had swept through the woods and uprooted a number of trees.

Boomer shouted, "Give me a hand, Little Bro!"

Cody reluctantly left his imaginary village and jogged to his brother.

Boomer kicked a fallen tree trunk. "Help me move this."

Cody shook his head. He knew better than to ask why his brother wanted to move the tree trunk. He walked and stood next to Boomer. They pressed their hands against the decaying bark and drove forward with their legs. Grunting, straining they were able to move the log a few inches.

Boomer dropped to his knees and scooped dirt from beneath the tree.

Cody said, "Watch out for snakes."

Boomer quipped in mock terror, "Snakes."

"And spiders."

Boomer added sarcastically, "Anything else, Mom."

Boomer filtered clumps of dirt through his fingers. He dug further beneath the log and scooped again. Peering intently, he shifted the dirt.

"Whoa!"

Cody leaned over his shoulder. "What do ya got?"

Boomer gently brushed dirt with his fingertips then held the object up to the sun. Imbedded in dirt were two arrowheads fused together. The arrow shafts had deteriorated ages ago. He tried to pry the arrowheads apart with his stubby fingers.

"No, I'll break it." He passed the arrowheads to Cody. "You do it."

"What, it's OK for me to break them."

Cody carefully examined the arrowheads, then got up and ran across the bluff and slid down the embankment to the river. Boomer raced in his footsteps.

Cody kneeled next to the river. He swirled and rubbed the arrowheads in the water.

"You got your pocket knife?"

Boomer took his knife from his jeans pocket, opened the knife and handed it to his brother.

Cody tried to pry the arrowheads apart. The knife slipped and nicked his thumb. He held his hand up as blood seeped from the cut.

Boomer said, "Hey, be careful. We're already blood brothers."

Cody laughed, then rinsed his thumb in the river. Carefully he slipped the knife's edge between the two arrowheads and wiggled the blade. The arrowheads broke apart. He washed one and then the other in the river then handed the arrowheads and the knife to his brother.

Boomer slid the knife back into his pocket, then took the arrowheads.

"Wow," Boomer said with a tone of reverence. "They're beauts." He held one arrowhead out to his brother. "Here."

Pressing his cut thumb with his finger to stem the bleeding, Cody took the arrowhead with his other hand.

Boomer asked, "How old do you think they are?"

"They got to be at least a couple hundred years old, maybe a lot older." Cody could feel the past in his hand. "Indians have been camping on these bluffs...for as long as there have been Indians in the forest."

"The arrowheads have been here all that time just waiting for us to find them."

"A talisman."

Boomer's eyebrows arched. "What's that?"

"An object that has magical powers."

"You mean," Boomer's white teeth flashed in a grin, "a lucky charm."

"Yeah," Cody met his brother's smile. "That too."

Boomer rubbed the arrowhead with his thumb, then slid it into his shirt pocket. He jumped up and yelled an Indian war cry. Birds flew squawking from the trees. He ran and splashed into the river, then jumped from stepping stone to stepping stone and climbed up onto Buffalo Rock.

The sunlit forest behind him and swirling rapids at his feet, he stood tall on the boulder and raised his fists in the air.

Cody stared at his brother. He closed his hand around his arrowhead and held it next to his chest.

CHAPTER 20

The air was still. Water rippled. The sun slowly sank beneath tree tops casting crimson cottony streaks across the cobalt blue sky. Cody sat next to his brother, their legs dangling over the side of Buffalo Rock. Each brother was lost in his own thoughts, his own feelings.

"I'm going, Little Bro."

Cody tried to steel himself. He knew what was coming. On the way back from the airport when Boomer didn't tell him where he was going to be stationed, he knew then where Boomer was going. He ignored it like he refused to think about school during Christmas vacation.

Cody swallowed and tried to find his voice. "Do you even know why we're over there, because I don't."

"What's to know?"

His brother's flippant attitude suddenly made Cody angry. Almost like a slap he said, "Boomer."

Boomer's face took on a seriousness that Cody seldom saw.

"I don't need to know why we're over there. My country says they need me in Iraq, that's where I'm going."

Every muscle in Cody's body tensed in frustration. He said resignedly, "My country right or wrong."

"And what's wrong with that?" Boomer swept his arm encompassing the river and woods. "Look around you, this is our country."

Cody didn't answer. He knew there were some arguments with Boomer he could never win. He hugged his legs to his chest and rested his chin on top of his knees.

Boomer didn't want to spend his last night on leave arguing with his brother. He playfully cupped the back of Cody's neck and shook him. "I'm starving. Let's go into town and get something to eat."

Saturday night all the parking spots were filled on Main Street. Boomer ended up parking down by Promenade Park. They walked the sidewalk up to Laura's Restaurant. As they passed the Photo Shop, Cody looked in the window and saw Kim behind the counter.

Cody stopped and said, "Why don't you get a table. I'll catch up with you in a minute."

Boomer paused trying to figure out what Cody was doing. He glanced in the window and then to his brother. A smile of recognition filled his face. Teasing he said, "No way." He wagged his head while backing away on the sidewalk.

Fifteen minutes later, Cody opened the door for Kim that led into Laura's Restaurant. The place was wall to wall with people in the entranceway, every table taken. It seemed like everyone was glancing to the corner where Boomer stood like he was holding court, jesting, telling stories. After breaking the news to him, Cody knew Boomer had told someone else he was going to Iraq. The word had quickly spread from person to person, table to table.

Boomer saw Cody and waved. Cody motioned Kim to follow him. He tried to cleave his way through the crowd. When he reached Boomer, he turned back, but he couldn't see Kim. He started to fight his way back to the door. He felt a hand on his arm stop him. He turned and almost magically Kim appeared in front of Boomer.

Kim said, "What took you so long."

Cody felt his face relax in a smile. Boomer towered over Kim. He sometimes forgot how gigantic his brother is standing 6 foot 5 and over 260 pounds. Kim seemed like a little kid.

The hostess called Boomer's name. The owner had moved Boomer from the bottom of the waiting list to the top.

Boomer clapped his hands and shouted, "All right."

For a second, Cody was afraid Boomer was going to scoop Kim up and carry her on his shoulder above the crowd to the dining room.

Cody sat next to Kim across from Boomer, but they never really had a chance to talk. There was a constant procession of people stopping at their table. One group would finish their meal and stop on their way out, the other group would stop on the way to the empty table. Some of the people they knew since they were kids others were just nodding acquaintances. It didn't matter if Boomer was eating, they'd still stop and talk. Boomer would nod - or worse, talk with his mouth full of food.

They all wanted to wish him well and to touch him. Men would slap Boomer on the shoulder or shake his hand. Woman would caress his fingers or make Boomer blush when they kissed his cheek.

The food never stopped. An empty dessert plate would be replaced with a full one.

As the evening went on Cody was overwhelmed. He never expected such an outpouring of support for his brother. Boomer took it all in stride with an unflappable smile for everyone. Kim seemed enthralled with all the attention directed at Boomer. Cody felt a tinge of envy and jealousy.

The dinner rush came and went. Finally they had a moment alone. Boomer reached into his shirt pocket and said, "Kim, check this out." He set the arrowhead on the table. "Cody's got one just like it. We found them together."

Cody set his arrowhead next to Boomer's.

Kim asked, "Where did you find them?"

Beaming like a kid showing off his prized treasure, Boomer said, "In the woods above Buffalo Rock."

Kim took Cody's arrowhead, turned it over in her hand and studied it. "It's way cool."

Boomer snatched his arrowhead and slid it back in his pocket. "I'm taking it with me. Cody says it's a talisman." Boomer stood and stretched. "Aw man, been sitting too long. We better get going."

Kim handed the arrowhead to Cody who slid it into his pocket.

In the truck on the way home Boomer was whistling. It was one of Boomer's traits, especially when he was happy, he would whistle. Sometimes Cody would recognize the song but most times it was like Boomer was making up his own music. It was always a happy tune.

Cody leaned back in the seat and let the day sink in; the hunting for arrowheads, the view from Buffalo Rock, the dinner with Boomer and Kim.

Almost like reading his thoughts, Boomer said, "What a perfect day," then went back to whistling.

When the boys got home, the lights were on in the front room. Cody was first through the front door. His mother was sitting in her chair by her reading lamp. Soon as Cody saw her face he knew someone who had been at Laura's Restaurant called and mentioned Iraq. His dad came in from the TV room.

There was such a sharp contrast between his parents' expressions. His mother looked angry but at the same time like she was doing everything she could to keep from crying. His father looked anxious, but also proud.

Boomer had a bewildered, befuddled expression on his face. The one where he knew he was in trouble but wasn't sure how to get out of it. He turned to Cody for help. Cody shrugged his shoulders. He knew this was something Boomer had to face alone. He bounced up the stairs, leaving his brother behind.

CHAPTER 21

Eileen shouted from the bottom of the stairs, "Are you up, Cody!"

Cody tried to catch the tail end of his dream, but it slipped away.

"Cody!"

He shouted, "I'm up." He slid his feet to the hardwood floor, then sat on the edge of the bed.

Eileen said, "Are you sure you're up?"

"Yes!"

"I'll see you tonight."

He mumbled, "Bye, Mom," but doubted that she heard him. He fought the urge to lie down again. He pushed off the bed and headed to the shower.

Eileen had set the box of Cheerios and a banana by his bowl on the table before she left for 7:00 a.m. Mass at St. Patrick's. She started going to Mass every day when Boomer left for Iraq.

Cody grabbed the milk from the refrigerator and sat at the table. While eating his cereal he scanned the paper, not the local *Grand Rapids Gazette* that came out once a week, but the paper from the city that was printed daily. He searched for any article on the war in Iraq, but like most days he found nothing. Cody thought if people read just the paper they wouldn't even know there was still a war going on in Iraq. He could turn on the TV, but that was even worse. TV was entertainment, celebrities, fashion, weather, sports, but no coverage on Iraq or Afghanistan.

He set his bowl in the sink, grabbed the keys to Boomer's truck, then tapped his pants front pocket, feeling the reassuring outline of the arrowhead. He headed off to school.

After English class, Cody told Kim the only daily coverage he could find on the war in Iraq and Afghanistan was on the internet. He felt like there was a conspiracy to keep him in the dark about what was happening over there.

Kim said, "You need to talk with my grandfather."

Cody asked, "Why?"

"Stop by the shop after football practice." Kim rushed off to her next class.

Cody wondered if Kim intentionally created some of the air of mystery that seemed to surround her. She not only didn't answer his question, she also left him wondering why she didn't answer it.

The bells jingled when Cody opened the door to the Photo Shop. Kim stuck her head out of the storage room, then waved Cody back.

Kim was on a step stool trying to wrestle a cardboard box down from the wooden shelves built next to the wall. Cody couldn't help staring at the back of her jeans.

Kim turned and caught him staring. "Hey…"

Cody's eyes drifted to the mischievous smile on her face.

"I could use some help here."

"Let me get it."

Cody moved forward and put his hands next to Kim's on the box. For the first time they were eye to eye. Cody closed his mouth. He wished he had brushed his teeth or at least chewed a mint. Kim's coffee eyes were playful, toying. Cody felt paralyzed. He could feel her warm breath on his cheek. Kim closed her eyes. He leaned and brushed her lips with his and it was like a soft current flowed all the way down to his toes.

Bells jingled. It took Cody a second to realize it was the front door.

Kim's eyes sprang open. She whispered, "Grandfather." She jumped off the step stool and went over to the work table. "Bring it over here."

Cody set the cardboard box on the table. Kim lifted the lid revealing the photographs.

Mr. Lewinski walked by the storage room. Surprised to see Cody with Kim, he said, "What are you two up to?"

Kim said, "I wanted to show Cody some of the photographs from Vietnam." She lifted photos from the box and arranged them on the table. Some of the photos were 8 by 10, others snapshots. Some were cut out of newspapers and magazines and pasted on cardboard. "At school Cody was talking about how there is so little coverage on the war in Iraq. I thought maybe you could...I don't know...maybe compare it to Vietnam."

"It was a different time, a different war, Kim."

Kim lifted a photo of a Marine in a fox hole. His face was smeared with mud and blood. He was staring at the camera with a vacant, haunting, shell-shocked expression.

"Did you take this photo?"

Stanley moved closer to the table and looked at the picture.

"No, that's one of Larry Burrows'. He shot almost all of his photos in color. I mainly used black and white." Stanley pulled a vivid color photo of a helicopter spewing flames dropping from the sky. "Larry covered most of the war. I think he got there in '62. He was killed in Laos in 1971."

Cody said with a tone of incredulity, "You were in Vietnam?"

Stanley nodded. "I got there later, '69 and stayed to '72." He lifted a couple combat photos from the box. "These were taken by Catherine Leroy probably around '67. She'd go right into the thick of a firefight. She had a gift for faces."

Cody reached into the box and took out one of the newspaper photos.

"They printed these in the papers."

"A lot of our photos went out on the AP wire and were picked up by newspapers all over the country."

Cody asked, "Why don't we see pictures like these ... today ... in our paper?"

"You sound like one of my students at the U." Stanley brushed his hand through his thick white mustache. "It always comes back to money. It takes a lot of money to keep journalists in the field, especially in Iraq and Afghanistan. Papers cut expenses by cutting their personnel. Fewer journalists, fewer stories. As news coverage diminished so did the public's interest in the war."

Stanley lifted a photo of an Army squad on patrol in the jungles of Vietnam. "Part of the reason now is war fatigue. People are tired of the war. They don't want to hear about it on their nightly newscast." Stanley let the photo slide through his fingers. "And then there's the government. They don't want Americans to become disheartened by seeing their sons and daughters coming home in body bags."

Cody said, "But, it's not right."

"One of the main reasons why the Vietnam War ended was because the American public said, 'Enough.'" Mr. Lewinski searched through the photo box. He handed a photo to Cody. "Chuck Harrity took this picture in '73. The baby sleeping in the cardboard box, that was her home and the young boy lying next to her on the cement, was her brother who begged on the streets of Saigon for food for him and his baby sister. Photos like these brought the reality of war home to the American public."

Cody could not imagine how difficult their lives must have been.

Stanley handed him another photo.

Shocked, Cody said, "This isn't real."

"Eddie Adams took that photo on the streets of Saigon in '68. The man with the gun was South Vietnam's National Police Brigadier General Nguyen Ngoc Loan. Right there on the street he pulled out his gun and summarily executed a captured Viet Cong officer." Stanley pointed. "You can see the bullet coming out of his head."

Cody stared at the photo but it was so hard to comprehend that what he was holding actually happened.

Stanley took back the photo. "If there was one photo that defined the war and brought it to a close it had to be this." He gave Cody an eight by ten black and white photo. "South Vietnamese photographer Nick Ut took this shot outside the village of Trang Bang in '72. In the background you can see smoke and fire from the napalm attack. The young naked girl running towards the camera and screaming in excruciating pain was Kim Phuc."

Cody jerked his head to Kim. Reassured that she was still there and OK, he looked back to the photo.

Stanley continued, "You can't really see the burns in the picture. The napalm dropped during the air attack landed mainly on the young girl's back. The gel adhered and bored into her skin. She tore off her flaming, burning clothes."

The photo was so captivating Cody felt the girl's awful pain and heard her screams.

"Did she die?"

"No. Remarkably she didn't. Kim Phuc became a living memorial to the horrors of war."

The front door bells jingled. Stanley held his hand up stopping Kim. "I'll get it. It's probably Mrs. Albright. She was going to stop in tonight to pick up her pictures."

When Stanley left, Cody said, "This is unbelievable. I knew there was a war in Vietnam, but I didn't know it was so ...real." He looked at Kim. "And your grandfather was there."

Kim walked over to the storage shelves. She moved the step stool, jumped up and took a photo album from the shelf. She set the album on the table, then rapidly fanned through the photos to the back of the album. Over her shoulder, Cody could see flickering images of war. Kim stopped at pictures of a Vietnamese village. Some of the huts were on fire, others blown apart by mortars. Heavily armed American soldiers were searching the huts. Kim turned the page to the last photos in the album. In the shadows inside one of the huts, Cody saw four bodies. Three of the villagers were obviously dead. The next shot was a close-up of the fourth. A teenage girl was clutching her arm. In the photo her blood appeared black. Something was familiar about the girl's face. Cody glanced up and studied Kim and realized who it was.

"Your Grandmother."

Kim nodded and pointed at the other villagers in the photo. Her voice grew wistful. "That was my great-grandfather, my great-grandmother and my grandmother's sister. They were all killed. Grandfather tied a tourniquet on grandmother's arm then carried her to an aid station. They had to amputate her arm. In the hospital no one came to visit her. All her relatives were killed or missing. Grandfather would stop back and check on her and bring her gifts. They fell in love. He brought Grandmother here to Grand Rapids. He wanted to get her as far away from war as he could."

Kim closed the album. "That was the last combat photograph Stanley Lewinski ever took."

CHAPTER 22

The corn stalks were taller than Cody. The harvest moon bathed the cornfield in a soft golden light. A cool evening breeze rattled husks. Peals of laughter and shrieks of surprise echoed through the maze. Cody entwined his arm through Kim's. They both held flashlights, the beams sweeping the corn maze.

Feet pounded rapidly behind the cornstalks, then Cody recognized Chad's scream, "Got cha. Freeze!"

A blended unison of, "Nooooo!" Cody pictured another couple frozen by Chad's flashlight.

Cody pulled Kim deeper into the maze. They turned a corner. Cody snapped his flashlight off. Kim snapped hers off. They stood waiting for their eyes to adjust to moonlight their matching breaths a nervous excited pitter-patter. Kim squeezed his arm as Cody slowly moved along the pathway.

Cody stopped at the next bend. He peered around the cornstalks. Sweeping yellowish-brown beams were coming toward them. He gently pushed Kim back into the cornstalks.

He leaned and breathed into her ear. "Wait for my light then turns yours on." As he kissed her ear, he could feel Kim tremor. He backed into the passageway then slid into the corn across from her. He could barely see her just the moonlight reflected in her eyes and the crescent smile of her teeth.

Twin beams swept the pathway. With each step closer, Cody's heart beat faster. He searched for Kim. He could see her eyes, but not her smile. The flashlight beams swept the cornfield. He froze, trying to become invisible as the beam passed over him. Light swept the other side. He caught a fleeting glimpse of Kim in the shadows, then the light moved on. When the couple was close enough for Cody to reach out and touch he screamed, "Booo!" and snapped his light on. Instantaneously Kim turned hers on. The girl screamed and the boy almost jumped out of his skin.

Cody sprang into the pathway. The couple's expressions were hilarious. Cody laughed so hard his flashlight jiggled all over the cornfield. Kim came out of the cornstalks her eyes teared from laughing. According to the rules, the couple was now frozen and needed to point their flashlights up to the autumn sky until the game was over.

Cody grabbed Kim's hand and they raced down the path. They rounded the bend and before he could stop, they ran right into the light beam. He froze and Kim bumped into him. He tried to see who was behind the harsh light. He recognized Ashley and heard Chad's snicker. Cody flipped his flashlight up in surrender. Ashley and Chad ran off.

Kim handed him her flashlight, then rubbed her hands up and down her arms.

Cody asked, "You cold?"

"A little bit."

Cody slipped her flashlight into his pocket. He wrapped an arm around her shoulders and drew her next to his chest.

"You're shivering. Come on I'll take you home."

"No. The game's not over." She nestled closer. "Just hold me, I'll be fine."

Cody searched the sky. A half-dozen beams like spotlights rose up from the corn maze. Shouts rang from the south end of the cornfield. Then all was quiet. One by one, the lights were lowered.

Kim said, "I wonder who won?"

Cody laughed. "Chad, Chad always wins."

With a nervous titter, Kim asked, "You do know how to find the way back?"

"We just follow the breadcrumbs."

Kim smacked his chest.

"Ouch. That hurt."

Kim rubbed where she smacked him then grabbed hold of his waist. She rested her face next to his torso. Looking like they were joined together they slowly walked the pathway.

Kim asked, "Did anyone ever get lost in here?"

"You are scared."

Kim held him tighter. "Don't you think it's spooky?"

"Nah." He leaned and kissed her hair. The way she clung to him made him feel brave, that he could protect her from anything.

The players gathered at the entrance to the corn maze. Everyone wanted to play again.

Cody looked at Kim, who stood with her arms tight to her chest, her lips quivering.

He said, "You guys go."

Chad said, "One more game. Just one."

Cody shook his head. "Nah. Next time." He draped his arm over Kim and headed to the parking lot.

"You're making me feel bad. I know you wanted to play again," said Kim

"You're still shaking."

Her teeth chattering Kim said, "I should have brought a coat."

They got in the truck. Cody started the engine and turned on the heater.

"It'll be warm in a minute."

He rested his hands on the steering wheel and gazed at the cornfield. Flashlights darted through the maze. He suddenly thought about Boomer and wondered what his brother was doing on the other side of the world. He reached into his pant's pocket and brought out the arrowhead. He rubbed the flint between his thumb and forefinger. Flashlight beams lit the corn like streaks of fire.

Kim turned up the fan and warm air engulfed the cab.

"Are you OK?"

Cody shrugged. "I was just thinking about, Boomer." He slid the arrowhead back in his pocket then dropped the truck in gear.

CHAPTER 23

Many things changed in the Brennans house when Boomer joined the army, but not the tradition of Sunday dinner. During the school year, Cody was free to set his own schedule, but on Sunday evenings at 6, he would sit at the dining room table and breathe in the rich aroma of baking breads and roasting meat with his mouth watering and his stomach doing anticipatory cartwheels. Eileen would cook a meal with enough leftovers to last through the week. Depending on her mood it might be ham, turkey, or pot roast. There would always be some sort of potatoes, and plenty of vegetables. The desert pies would change with the seasons, pumpkin, mince meat, apple, cherry, peach cobbler.

Sunday dinner was one of the few times Cody would see his dad during the week. Between school and football, and Jack working 12-hour days running the construction business, their paths rarely crossed. His father made a point of going to all his Friday night games. Cody would see his mother and father in the bleachers, but they usually left right after the game and would be in bed by the time he got home. Sunday dinner was a time to catch up on what happened during the week. They'd talk about Cody's football game, Jack's latest remodel. Eileen was mostly a silent observer content to let her boys talk. Cody would find ways to talk around Kim.

The kitchen wall phone rang. Conversation stopped and they all stared at the ringing phone that seemed so out of place on a Sunday evening. Anyone who would call Cody always called his cell. The front parlor was remolded into an office and any work- related calls would ring in on the office phones or on Jack's cell.

Eileen voiced their shared concern, "I wonder who's calling?"

"I bet you it's Boomer," said Jack.

He pushed back from the table and hustled to the phone.

"Yes, this is Mr. Brennan."

Jack's lips compressed into a tight line, his face went pale and then flushed beet red. He looked at Cody and made a frantic scribbling motion with his hand.

Cody got up so fast he knocked his chair over. He opened the junk drawer and snatched a pen. He couldn't find any paper so he pulled the calendar off the refrigerator and set it on the counter by his dad.

"I don't understand … my son is not in Iraq?" Gulping words, Jack continued, "You're saying Boomer's in the Brooke Army Medical Center. Where's that?" Jack pressed the phone to his ear with his shoulder as he tried to write on the calendar but the words came out as squiggles.

Eileen appeared at Jack's side with a pen and notepad.

"You need our permission to operate….I…I…"

Eileen said with a still, no nonsense voice, "Give me the phone." She took the phone from her husband. "This is Mrs. Brennan. Who am I speaking with…"

Beads of perspiration covered Jack's forehead. He walked and sank into his chair at the table. He tugged on his shirt collar his breath bellowing.

"Are you OK, Dad?"

Jack shooed the question away. He lifted the water glass and took small sips.

Cody's eyes swung frantically back and forth between his mother and father. Eileen's back was to them. Cody strained to hear what she was saying, but caught only fragments as she filled page after page in the notepad. "Think is best …Yes… Yes…Survival rate… operate…burn unit…"

Cody knew if he didn't run to the bathroom he would pee his pants.

When he came back to the kitchen his mother was sitting at the table holding Jack's hand. He took his seat and his mother's other hand found his.

Chapter 24

Cody's mind was racing and he couldn't get it to slow down. They were in the SUV somewhere in Indiana. His father was driving and he was sitting next to him. Eileen was in the back seat. The car was quiet except for the hum of tires on the expressway and the clicking of his mother's rosary beads.

Boomer was hurt. They didn't know how badly. From what he could get out of his mother, one of the Humvees in the convoy was hit with an IED, an improvised explosive device. His brother was air evacuated to Landstuhl Medical Center in Germany and from there flown to the Burn Unit at Brooke Army Medical Center in San Antonio, Texas. As they drove, Boomer was undergoing surgery. The doctors didn't want to wait for them to get there, saying the longer they waited the greater the risk for infection.

Cody's heart was pounding. He checked the overhead road signs as they drove by an exit on the expressway. He flicked on a small flashlight and studied the printouts he got off the internet.

After the phone call, his dad checked on flights out of Detroit to San Antonio. The earliest they could have left would be the next afternoon. Cody used MapQuest to check routes to San Antonio on his computer and found if they drove straight through they would make better time in the SUV. They quickly packed and were on the road.

Cody said, "Take 70 west, Dad."

Jack nodded. His face appeared ashen in the glow of the overhead highway lights. Cody wondered if his father had a panic attack - or worse yet a minor heart attack - back at the house. He seemed OK now or at least as OK as he could be under the circumstances.

Cody turned and looked at his mom.

Eileen asked, "You want a pop?"

"Yeah."

Eileen took a Coke from the cooler. "How about a sandwich?"

"No. Just a Coke."

His mother surprised him. He always thought his father would be the one who could handle any crisis, but it was his mother who stepped forward and took charge. She knew what needed to be done and assigned everyone some tasks. She was so efficient, Cody thought it was almost like she had planned everything out in advance.

"You want some coffee, Jack?"

Jack nodded.

Cody checked his printouts. With luck they could be in San Antonio by late tomorrow afternoon. He would give anything right now to have Internet access. There were so many things he could be looking up instead of just staring out the window at the seemingly endless mile markers.

Cody woke with a jolt. He opened his eyes to sunshine. It was a few seconds before he realized he was in the SUV headed to Texas. He didn't remember falling asleep. Suddenly he felt guilty as if he let his father down.

He snatched the printouts from the console. "Where are we?"

Jack answered, "Coming up to Little Rock."

"Arkansas?"

"Yeah. We're almost on empty. We need to fill up."

Cody realized he had been sleeping for the last four hours. Crestfallen he said, "I'm sorry...I didn't mean to fall asleep."

"There's nothing to be sorry for. You needed to get some sleep."

"I can drive after we fill up. Then you can sleep for awhile."

"There's no way I'm going to be able to sleep, I'm too wired from all the coffee."

They stopped at one of the large truck stops that line the highway exits. Cody and Jack switched off - one filling the SUV while the other used the restroom. Ten minutes later they were back on the highway. Jack still wanted to drive but Eileen overrode him.

Cody drove. His dad sat up front with him. He didn't know if it was because his dad was up all night, but when Cody looked at him he seemed old.

They switched drivers again in Texas. The closer they got, the more anxious Cody became. He knew he wasn't alone. He could feel his mother's and father's trepidation through Jack's constant drumming of fingers on the steering wheel and Eileen's whispered prayers.

They parked in the visitors' lot of the Burn Unit of Brooke Army Medical Center. The word *burn* stood out, stark, by itself, conveying nightmare images that raced through Cody's mind.

CHAPTER 25

The nurse, Captain Driscoll, said, "Private Brennan is out of surgery. Right now his condition is stable."

Cody clung to the word *stable* like it was a lifeline to his brother. They were in a waiting room on the fourth floor of a burn unit. The nurse was dressed in military fatigues, his hair a crew cut, his demeanor professional but his eyes seemed too old for his chiseled face.

Jack intoned, "Do you know what happened."

Captain Driscoll pointed to the table. He waited until everyone took a seat and then continued. "From the reports we have coming in from the field your son's unit was on patrol south of Baghdad. The lead Humvee was hit by an IED. Two soldiers were killed in the explosion. Three soldiers were trapped in the wreckage that was engulfed in flames. Private Brennan was in the following Humvee. You son sustained burns when he entered the lead Humvee and pulled three soldiers from the wreckage. One of the soldiers died in the field. Another died on the flight from Landstuhl. The last soldier is in surgery. His wounds are more catastrophic. Besides the burns, he sustained massive injuries from the explosion."

Jack said, "Good Lord."

Eileen asked, "Can we see our son?"

Captain Driscoll paused as if debating how to continue. "Your son's third degree burns are mainly on his hands and face."

Eileen gave an involuntary gasp. She quickly covered her mouth.

Cody blanched. He felt lightheaded. He lowered and clutched his head between his palms.

Captain Driscoll said, "I know this is a shock, but Private...

Eileen interrupted, "Boomer. Everyone calls him Boomer."

Captain Driscoll opened the medical chart and wrote Boomer by Private Jack Brennan Jr.

"Boomer's vitals are strong. Our main concern is infection. When he arrived here he underwent a cleaning process called debridement to remove any dead skin. During surgery, the team of doctors cut away the remaining dead tissue to reduce the risk of infection and then they began a series of skin grafts. Boomer's most serious full thickness burns occurred on exposed body areas. His body armor protected his torso. We can take future skin grafts from his stomach."

Captain Driscoll noticed how pale Cody had become. "Son, do you want a drink of water?"

Cody swallowed and shook his head.

"Pain management is critical. Boomer is sedated and will be for a while. There was some damage to his lungs and as a precautionary measure he is on a ventilator."

Captain Driscoll closed Boomer's file. He sat back and looked at the Brennans.

"I know right now you are feeling overwhelmed, but Boomer has a lot of positives. He's young and strong." His eyes met Jack's, "I know he is a fighter. His burns are localized." Captain Driscoll pointed to the doorway. "We have some soldiers in the ward who have suffered burns to over 95% of their bodies. Boomer's road ahead is going to be difficult. Skin grafts and reconstructive surgery take time. Rehabilitation is a very painful process…"

Her lower lip quivering, Eileen said, "I want to see my son."

Captain Driscoll consolingly said, "I know Mrs. Brennan, give me a few more minutes then we will go to the ward."

Eileen lowered her eyes to Boomer's chart.

"Right now your son's greatest risk is infection. When we go into the ward we need to gown up; caps, masks, gowns, booties. You are going to find the ward very warm. The temperature is kept at over 90 degrees. Because of their burns and subsequent skin loss many of the soldiers have lost the ability to regulate their body temperatures. That's why the ward needs to be kept warm."

The nurse paused. His eyes lingered on Eileen, then Jack and then Cody. He continued with an underlying tone of pain and sadness. "Right now there are about 40 soldiers in the ward, some of their burns are …you need to prepare yourself."

Captain Driscoll lifted Boomer's chart. He turned to Cody. "How old are you, son?"

"Seventeen."

"I'm going to take your mom and dad back first…"

"I want to see Boomer."

"You will, son, but first…"

"No."

Jack said, "Cody."

Cody slammed his hands on the table. He got up and walked to the windows. He pressed against the glass and stared at the empty blue sky.

In the waiting room there were two clocks on the wall. Cody checked his wristwatch but none of the three times were the same. He realized his wristwatch was set to Eastern Time and the one clock was set to local Texas time, but what was the other clock? It came to him when he thought about the internet and trying to get daily updates. The second clock was set to the time in Iraq.

He paced the waiting room, 10 steps turn, 10 steps turn, 10 steps turn... the seconds like minutes, the minutes like hours.

The door opened and his father entered the room. Jack's face was flushed and dripping perspiration. Eileen followed. Jack turned back to his wife.

Eileen went to him. She lifted her hands and pounded her fists against Jack's chest.

"What have you done to my boy?"

Jack stood still, then his large arms drew her to him.

His mother's sobs was the worst sound Cody ever heard.

CHAPTER 26

Sometimes before a football game Cody could tell how fast his heart was beating by looking at his fingertips. Today the beats were too quick to count. He was all thumbs trying to slip the sterile booties over his shoes. He was acutely aware of how bad he smelled from twenty-two hours in the SUV combined with nervous perspiration bordering on terror.

Captain Driscoll tied the strings for Cody's gown and adjusted his cap. He stared into Cody's eyes.

"You don't have to go back there."

Cody exhaled, trying to cleanse his fear. "Yes I do." He positioned the mask above his nose. The cloth clung to his mouth as he breathed in.

Beads of sweat popped like blisters on his face when they entered the ward. Everything appeared white and silver - white fluorescent lights, towels, gauze bandages beddings, silver bed-rails, ventilators, monitors, and gleaming instruments on surgical trays.

He followed Captain Driscoll down the long hallway hearing muted voices, the hum of machines and the rasp of ventilators. Some doorways were partially closed some wide open. Cody kept his eyes straight ahead focused on the back of Captain Driscoll's gown.

The nurse slowed and approached a soldier in a wheelchair. Cody's eyes drifted to the patient. It was like a nightmare where he wanted to scream but he couldn't, wanted to run but his legs wouldn't move. He blinked and blinked and blinked trying to awaken.

Captain Driscoll's face was inches from his eyes. The nurse took his arm and led him down the corridor.

From the doorway, Cody thought his brother was enclosed in a white cocoon. His body was covered by blankets, his hands and arms and head wrapped in gauze. The breathing tube disappeared into whiteness. Cody inched into the room listening to the rhythmic cadence of the ventilator.

Captain Driscoll checked the monitors by the side of the bed. Cody took one tentative step and then another. He stopped and stared in disbelief. There were no bandages around Boomer's eyes. His eyebrows were singed and his closed eyelids were surrounded by pink ovals.

Astonished, Cody said, "His eyes."

"Boomer was wearing goggles that protected his eyes and the skin under the goggles. We call it a reverse raccoon pattern because it looks like the opposite of raccoon eyes. The goggles saved his eyesight." The nurse checked the bandages on Boomer's arms. "I wish he had been wearing FR gloves."

To Cody, Boomer's hands looked like claws under the gauze. "FR?"

"Flame resistant. Hand burns are devastating. The skin is so thin and sensitive." He held his hand palm up in front of Cody. "You can't use skin grafts on the palm." He turned his hand over and rubbed his knuckles. "There's no fat. Burns cripple the tendons and the top of the fingers are just skin."

Cody moved closer to the bed. He wanted to touch his brother. He needed the physical contact. Tentatively he moved his fingers to Boomer.

"You can rest your hand on his chest."

Cody gently set his open palm on his brother's chest. He could feel the strong heartbeat beneath the rise and fall of his hand.

"When will he wake up?"

"Right now it's better for Boomer just to sleep."

A monitor sounded in the next room. The nurse backed away from the bed.

"I need to check on another patient. Will you be OK for a little while?"

Cody whispered, "Yeah."

"Talk to your brother."

Cody turned to the nurse. "But, he can't hear me."

"Are you sure?" asked Captain Driscoll.

Cody gazed back to his brother and the nurse left the room.

Boomer's eyebrows were arched like they were frozen in a moment of surprise or panic. The outsides of his eyes were deeply wrinkled as if he was squeezing his eyes shut.

Next to Boomer's eyes, Cody saw charred skin under the gauze. The enormity of what was concealed under Boomer's bandages suddenly hit him harder than any linebacker. He had no idea what to say to his brother. With a heartrending cry he said, "Oh, Boomer."

His brother's eyelids remained shut but Cody felt Boomer's eyes move towards him.

His voice cracking, he said "It's going to be OK."

One hand rested on his brother's heart, his other hand wiped flowing tears.

CHAPTER 27

Cody learned there was time, and then there was hospital time. Back at home he would struggle to get out of bed in the morning only to find himself back in bed at night amazed at how quickly the day flew by.

Hospital time was waiting time. Boomer was off the respirator, but still sleeping. Cody and his parents took shifts so someone was always with Boomer. Cody sat by the bed and waited. Waited for his brother to wake up, waited for something, anything to happen. He felt like he was frozen in a time warp.

With nothing else to do, he started talking to Boomer. He went back to his childhood and took Boomer with him, back to riding bikes on dirt roads, canoeing on the river, shooting bb guns at tin cans, climbing trees in McQueen's orchard and shaking the branches to see who could get the most apples to fall, hauling a Christmas tree through snow back home from the woods. Some of the stories made him laugh and some made him feel like they were still kids. Boomer's body remained still but his closed eyes moved as if he were dreaming.

They met with Captain Driscoll and Boomer's team of surgeons. Cody tried to follow along as they explained procedures for skin grafts and reconstructive surgery. Boomer's case wasn't unique. Over the course of the war in Iraq, hundreds of soldiers were treated in the burn unit and many of them were able to return to duty. Boomer would need reconstructive surgery on his lips, nose and ears. The reconstruction along with skin grafts for his neck and face would involve a series of operations over the next couple of months. The surgeons explained what they hoped to accomplish, but stressed Boomer would never look the way he did before. He would be scarred for the rest of his life.

The surgeons were not as optimistic about Boomer's hands. There was the possibility that they would need to amputate one or both hands. It was too soon to assess nerve and tendon damage to know if he would regain any function in his fingers. Only time would tell. Without the use of his hands, Boomer would be dependent on others for his activities of daily living. He would need help with eating, bathing, dressing, and toileting.

The surgeons concluded their talks with pain management. Of all the wounds suffered in combat, pains from burns are the most excruciating and some of the necessary treatments make the pain worse. Changing the dressings and putting on antibiotic cream are necessary to fight off infection, but the pain can be unbearable. There is only so much that modern medicine can do to block pain.

Captain Driscoll stood by the monitors. He gathered the family together when Boomer showed signs of regaining consciousness.

Cody, his mother and father waited by the side of the bed. Everyone was dressed in matching sterile gowns with their faces hidden behind masks. Cody could see his parents' anxious concerned eyes. Jack kept dabbing the sleeve of his gown against his forehead trying to absorb his sweat.

Captain Driscoll said, "Many of our patients when they regain consciousness think they are still in Iraq."

Boomer was enveloped in a white cocoon except for his eyes. He stirred. His heart rate increased on the monitor. His eyes opened. A guttural feral sound rose from his chest. He tried to rise up from the bed. Captain Driscoll placed one hand on his chest. Boomer's confused panic stricken eyes darted around the room.

"Easy, Private. You're in a hospital back in the states."

Eileen leaned over her son her face inches from his eyes.

"Boomer, I'm here."

His eyes questioning, Boomer tried to focus on his mother. His jaw slightly moved beneath the gauze. His tongue rasped behind destroyed lips.

"Don't try to talk, son," said Captain Driscoll.

Suddenly Boomer's eyes grew wide. His body painfully convulsed as if jolted by electricity. As his body tightened one of the bandages pulled away revealing a stark blackened cheekbone. Captain Driscoll increased the pain medication flowing into the drip in Boomer's arm. His eyes closed and his body sank into the hospital bed.

Cody starred in horror at his brother's cheek knowing what was behind the rest of the bandages.

Cody stood by the window in the family waiting room. His face was covered with sweat and he couldn't seem to get enough air.

Sitting at the table, Eileen curled her hands around a paper coffee cup. Without make-up her skin looked lined and pale. She had puffy bags beneath her blue eyes. Her nose was red from the countless tissues she used over the last couple of days.

Her face was set like she made a decision. She looked across the table at her husband and said, "I want you and Cody to go home."

Jack protested, "Eileen."

"Boomer is going to be here for months."

Jack said, "Then we'll stay for months."

Everything was wrong and there was nothing Cody could do about it. Boomer...his parents arguing ... he wanted to scream, he wanted to throw things, he wanted to smash his hand through the window. All of the sudden it was too much. He ran across the room and yanked open the door. He raced down the hall to the exit. He ran down the stairs. His feet thumped as he jumped to the landings on each floor.

Eileen turned on her husband. Her pent-up anger, hurt and worry lashed out.

"Don't you see what this is doing to Cody? Isn't Boomer's pain enough!"

Jack recoiled as if Eileen slapped him

As soon as she said the words she wanted to take them back.

"I didn't mean that." She stood and cradled Jack's face. "I'm sorry." She waited for her breathing to slow.

"Please, Jack, take Cody home. I'll stay here with Boomer."

Cody burst out of the entrance of the burn center. He ran. He had no idea where he was going. He followed the road leading away from the hospital running as fast as he could.

CHAPTER 28

Cody didn't realize how much he missed Kim until he saw her. She was standing, waiting by his parking spot at school. When he got out of Boomer's truck she didn't say anything. She walked up to him wrapped her arms around his waist and leaned her head on his chest. Cody rested his chin on top of her head and just held her.

As Kim and Cody walked the hallway to class students fell silent. Everyone knew Boomer was injured in Iraq, but no one knew what to say. When they passed by hushed conversations rippled in their wake.

Cody found it hard to concentrate. In English he kept reading the same paragraph over and over again not finding any meaning to the words. In social studies the teacher's voice was like background music.

One school day blended into another. Cody occupied space in the classrooms, but his mind was a thousand miles away.

Cody blew on his hands. Snowflakes sparkled in the stadium lights. It was way too cold for November and the last game of the season. He reached under center, grabbed the football, quickly took a three step drop then fired a dart to Chad over the middle.

The referee raised his hands. The Generals fans cheered. Cody jogged to the sideline as his team set up for the extra point. He stood by Coach Stutz on the sideline letting the Coach's huge body block the wind.

The extra point was good. Generals 35, Blue Devils 17 with 1:05 left in the game. The Generals kicked off and tackled the Titans' running back at their own 35-yard line.

The clock ticked down and Cody slowly came out of the zone. When he played, he went completely into the game. There wasn't room for anything else in his mind but blitzing linebackers and his receivers' routes.

He wanted the game to go on. He wanted to stay in the zone.

Time ran out. The team ran from the field and huddled on the sideline. Cody felt the zone slip away as snowflakes melted on his hand. He turned to the bleachers. His father was standing alone. Cody jogged to his teammates, his thoughts returning to Boomer.

Eileen would call every evening at 9. If Cody was home, he would sit at the kitchen table and wait with his father for the call. His mother was staying in the hotel near the Brooke Army Medical Center. She emailed Cody a list of things she needed. Cody and his father packed her clothes, some books and personal items and sent them by UPS to Texas.

Eileen would call from her hotel room and Jack would always answer the phone after the third ring. Jack had switched one of the office phones for the kitchen phone so he could put his wife on a speaker. They would sit at the kitchen table and talk. Cody tried to picture his mother sitting with them as they talked around the table.

Calling from her hotel room, Eileen could speak freely. Cody could tell what sort of day she had and in turn what sort of day Boomer had just from the way she said hello. Over the past month, one operation led to another and if someone asked Cody how many skin grafts Boomer had, he couldn't say.

Tonight, Cody knew there was something wrong just from the tone of his mother's voice.

Eileen said, "The surgeons decided it would be best if they amputated...

There was a long pause and Cody thought for a second they'd lost the connection.

...three of Boomer's fingers on his left hand."

Jack gave an exasperated sigh and muttered, "Good Lord."

"The fingers were fused together in the fire. There was too much damage. He'll never regain their use. The doctors feel they can save Boomer's hand and with therapy he should regain the ability to use his thumb and index finger."

Jack asked, "Does Boomer know?"

"He wants them to do it. Boomer can't stand not being able to use his hands. I know how hard and frustrating it is for him when I feed him."

Cody unconsciously squeezed his hands. He pictured his mother spoon feeding his brother. He wondered who it was harder on - Boomer or his mother.

"They have started therapy on his right hand. By having the operation now, Boomer hopes they can do therapy on both hands at the same time."

"When will they do it?" Jack asked.

"The operation's scheduled for tomorrow morning."

Cody asked, "How's his ...." He wanted to ask about Boomer's face but he couldn't find the right words. "...you know the rest of him..."

"Boomer has a long way to go..." Eileen paused and Cody could picture his mother searching for words like he did. "They are able to take skin grafts from his body which is good because with foreign donors there is a higher risk of infection and rejection. Boomer calls the operations 'tummy tucks'..."

For the first time Cody felt a smile in his mother's voice.

"They've been taking grafts from his stomach. With each operation he ... looks better."

No one spoke. Cody tried to picture what his brother's face now looked like.

Eileen said, "Jack, I need you to send me my Christmas card list. It's in a folder in the file cabinet under C. And we need to talk about Christmas. I want you both to come here and we'll spend Christmas with Boomer."

Jack said, "Of course." He looked at Cody, who nodded.

There was another pause in the conversation and Cody knew it was time to go upstairs. He pushed back from the table. Jack lifted the receiver cutting off the speaker phone. Up in his bedroom Cody couldn't hear the whispered words exchanged between his mother and father.

CHAPTER 29

Cody sat in a chair in the stark, white hospital room. Boomer sat on the edge of his hospital bed. Captain Driscoll was slowly unraveling bandages from Boomer's face. The nurse's back was blocking Cody's view of his brother. Captain Driscoll let the bandages fall to the floor then stepped away. Cody screamed.

Cody sprang up in bed. The room was dark except for moonlight creeping between slats of the window blinds. His chest was pounding as he wondered if he really screamed or if that was part of the dream. Sweat coated his face. He got out of bed and flipped on the light. He didn't want to be in the dark. He went back to bed and sat on the edge, clutched his hands to his stomach and rocked back and forth.

He didn't want to fall back asleep because he was too afraid he would have the same dream.

Cody desperately needed someone to talk to. Especially when they were younger, Boomer was his sounding board. He could ask his brother questions he would never ask anyone else. Boomer might kid him about some of his questions, but he would never laugh at him. Boomer's answers were based on his simplistic view of life and right or wrong. Cody didn't always agree with his brother, but he would always consider his point of view.

On serious issues he would talk with his mother. They'd sit out on the porch in warm weather or in wintertime in front of the fireplace, and talk about God and faith and what Cody wanted to do with his life.

On practical matters he would talk with his dad. Jack could find a way to fix whatever was broken. It didn't matter if it was a flat tire or a dislocated shoulder, his father would find a way to make it better.

Now he didn't have Boomer or his mother to talk with. And his dad seemed withdrawn, facing his own problems. He needed someone to talk with not so much to answer his questions but his fears.

They met Ashley and Chad at the mall and watched the latest Batman movie. Cody couldn't believe he dozed off during the show. A light snow was falling as they drove back to Grand Rapids. Cody was quiet and pensive.

Breaking into his thoughts, Kim said, "We might have a white Christmas." She lowered the window and tried to catch snowflakes. "Does it snow down in Texas?"

"I don't know."

She brought her hand back in covered with big puffy flakes that quickly melted. She licked her palm. The open fields and road were covered in a pristine white sheet that muffled all sound but the tires' hum.

Her voice buoyant, she said, "Let's go down to the river."

Cody slowly steered the gravel path to the bluffs above Buffalo Rock. He parked on the bluff's edge. The truck's lights illuminated the gleaming granite outcropping rising up from the dark swirling river. Snow gently fell from the heavens and melted as it touched water. Across the river tree branches were coated white. He shut off the engine. They both lowered their windows. Cold air filled the cab.

Whispering as if she was afraid to break the spell, Kim said, "It's so beautiful."

Cody knew how she felt. The tranquil scene was achingly beautiful. They sat enveloped in silence their breaths misting fog.

"Brrrrr." Kim powered up her window.

Cody raised his window and turned on the engine. Kim climbed over the center console and nested into his warmth. He shut off the lights. In darkness he inhaled the scent of lilacs from her hair. Her fingers light as feathers touched his cheek. Gradually as their eyes adjusted they could see Buffalo Rock through falling snow.

"I'll miss you at Christmas, but I'm glad you'll be with Boomer."

Cody pushed her hand away from his cheek.

Kim stared at him in the dimness of the cab.

"What's wrong?"

Cody shook his head.

Kim cupped his chin and pulled his face to her. "Tell me."

"I'm scared."

Cody turned away and stared out the side window.

"In the burn unit I saw a soldier in the ward. His face was… I don't want to see Boomer like that." His voice on the edge of tears, he whispered, "I don't know if I can see him."

Kim massaged the back of his neck as she pondered his words.

"Remember when I showed you the pictures of my grandmother in the hospital in Vietnam."

Still staring out the window, Cody nodded.

"There is a whole box of photos that Grandfather took at the hospital. Some of them are of villagers who were burned by napalm."

"Like Kim Phuc."

Kim nodded. "Napalm was used throughout Vietnam. During the air bombings the gel would explode on contact and stick to anything. It would adhere and burn through skin. The first time I saw the photos I was shocked. I could not ever imagine anything so horrific. How could anyone ever inflict such pain and suffering? I'd go through the box and then put it away only to pull it out and go through it again and again. One day Grandfather found me looking at the photos. I felt like I was caught looking at dirty pictures. I don't know what I expected him to do. He didn't get mad. He just asked me, 'what was I doing?' I didn't know what to say. How could I explain something I didn't understand? Grandfather set the photos back in the box then put the box up on the shelf."

Kim's silence pulled Cody to her. His eyes filled with hers.

"It wasn't until years later when I looked at the photos again that I realized I was searching for the faces under the scars."

CHAPTER 30

Cody drove past houses trimmed with glittering Christmas lights, twinkling reindeers on lawns, and snow covered Santas' sleighs caught in spotlights on rooftops. When he turned in his driveway the only lights on the Brennans' property were the sodium light above the garage and a light in the kitchen. He parked and quietly entered the house, knowing his dad was already in bed.

On the kitchen table were the unopened Christmas cards that came in today's mail. He carried the cards into the front room and set them in a box by his mother's chair. If his mother were home she'd arrange the cards on the mantle above the fireplace and along the shelves of the bookcases. This was the first year there wasn't a Christmas tree in the corner. The boys would hand pick and cut the pine tree from the woods behind their house. Eileen would spend an afternoon decorating the tree with miniature lights and ornaments that were older than Boomer. Tonight the room felt cold and barren. He turned off the light and went up to his room.

Cody sat in front of his computer with his hands clenched in his lap. He knew the Internet was a highway that could take him anywhere. He thought about what Kim said. How do you see the faces under the scars?

When the burn victim appeared on the screen he wanted to hit the escape key. He forced himself to stare at the monitor.

They took turns driving to the Brooke Army Medical Center. Neither Cody nor his dad wanted to spend a night in a hotel so they drove straight through. They left the snow and the cold behind. Cody was driving when they crossed into Texas. A faint light was breaking to the East.

Jack shifted his huge bulk trying to get comfortable on the passenger seat. They had been quiet most of the trip so Cody was surprised when his father said, "Your mom blames me and maybe she's right." Jack sighed. "Good Lord, how did this ever happen."

Cody realized his father was like himself and needed someone to talk with.

"It's not your fault, Dad."

"He didn't have to go. I should have listened to your mom and kept him home. Had him work with me."

"He wanted to go."

Jack vehemently said, "But I could have convinced him to stay."

Morning light filtered into the SUV. Jack opened his thermos and poured a cup of coffee.

"I don't know what to do. Give me a broken pipe, a leaky roof, hell give me a backed-up sewer, I can fix it." The cup shook with anger and frustration. "I can't fix, Boomer."

It was one of the few times Cody heard his father sound despondent and that worried him more than anything else.

"You spend your whole life praying that something like this would never happen and when it does what can you do?"

Trying to believe the words, Cody said, "He'll be OK, Dad."

Cody stood in men's restroom of the burn unit of Brooke Army Medical Center. He splashed water on his face, then gripped the steel sink and stared into the mirror. He willed a smile and tried to freeze it. He had to get it right. The most important thing was how he reacted when he saw his brother. He knew he only had one chance. He slipped the mask over his nose covering his mouth but not his eyes.

Boomer was still in the same room. The door was open. He heard his mother's and father's voices. He stopped outside the door. He had never been so scared in his life. He took a deep breath and held it. He stepped into the room. His parents fell silent.

Boomer was sitting up in bed. Cody looked at his bandaged hands then lifted his eyes to his brother's face. The lips didn't move. A voice he didn't recognize said, "Hey, Little Bro." But the eyes were the same.

"Hey, Boomer."

Cody knew it would have been different if he wasn't prepared. He took in the rest of Boomer's face. He couldn't help thinking of the pictures in an anatomy book where the skin was peeled away to reveal underlying muscles. Boomer's left ear was just a knob and his right ear was missing the earlobe. His head and face were hairless except for faint eyebrows. His skin was a splotchy mixture of white, brown and bright pink. Corded muscles stood out in his neck amid fresh skin grafts. His nose looked out of place amid the ravages of his cheeks and chin. It seemed healthy - almost normal. Then Cody realized it was a prostheses. The lips were misshaped and swollen.

Cody moved to the bed and left his fear behind. It was Boomer. Not a grotesque phantom from his nightmares, but his brother.

CHAPTER 31

On the ride home from San Antonio, Cody tried to leave the burn unit behind, to vanquish images of soldiers without limbs, to purge the hospital's antiseptic smell and to silence the painful murmurs.

He decided to ask Kim to go with him to the Andersons' Christmas party. He desperately wanted to be around his friends, to be surrounded by bright colorful lights and loud music. He wanted to laugh at silly jokes, to see smiling, happy faces and to dance with Kim.

A Canadian clipper carried a fresh inch of snow and a frigid blast of artic air to Grand Rapids. Kim looked like a Christmas present. She wore white knee-high boots, a red skirt, a white winter jacket and a long red and white striped stocking cap with matching gloves.

They parked at top of the Andersons' long driveway. Kim didn't wait for Cody to open the door. She climbed down from the truck then shrieked when the frigid air hit her. By the time Cody got out she was fast-walking down the driveway seeking the warmth of the Andersons' house. She shrieked again as she hit a patch of ice and her feet slipped out beneath her.

Cody half-ran half-slid down the driveway. "Are you OK?"

Kim bounced up. Her boots skated on ice. Flailing her arms, she tried to regain her balance. Cody rushed in. She grabbed his arm and they both tumbled.

Kim ended up on top of him. She laughed, "Fine help you are. You were supposed to keep me from falling."

He laughed. "Now what are we going to do?"

"It's toooooo cold." Kim gave a quick kiss to his cheek then pushed up off him. She stood with her feet close together for balance and extended her hand to help him up.

Cody said, "No way!" He rolled over on his knees then slowly stood. "Baby steps."

He inched closer to her and she held onto his arm. Looking like an old married couple they slowly shuffled down the driveway.

The Andersons' rec room was warm from the wood stove and body heat. Kim's eyes sparkled like Christmas lights above rosy cheeks. She left her stocking cap on and the red woolen tassel swayed on her back as she led Cody from one group to another chattering happily like a child in a toy store.

Cody kept touching her, his hand in her hand or on her arm trying to draw on her liveliness.

Kim's eyes filled with wonder as she gazed to the corner. "Look at the tree." She tugged Cody across the room. "It's gorgeous!"

Laughing and trying to mimic her voice, Cody said, "Gorgeous."

Kim playfully rolled her eyes. She shoved him in front of the tree then stepped back. "Wow!" She stepped in and tapped his chest. "Don't move!" She disappeared into the crowd.

Cody wasn't surprised when she returned with the digital camera from her purse. She lifted the camera and moved from spot to spot to frame the shot. Finally she said, "Smile."

The flash went off and Cody came forward.

Kim shouted, "Stop!" She shook her head with a look that said he had no idea what was going on. "Go back!" Using her finger she pointed to the exact spot where she wanted him then held her hand up for him to stop.

Cody froze.

Kim searched the crowd, then darted over and pulled Ashley back with her. Ashley was just a little taller than Kim. She checked the angle again then gave Ashley the camera. Kim walked over to Cody and wrapped her arm around his waist and leaned her stocking-covered head on his chest. Looking back at the camera, she said, "Smile." She could feel Cody's smile through his chest as the camera flashed.

"One more." She turned Cody to her and with her eyes laughing said, "Think Mistletoe." She draped her hands on his shoulders, rose up on her toes and closed her eyes. He lowered his head and they kissed.

With Ashley and Cody looking over her shoulder, Kim viewed the photos.

Ashley smiled, then turned and shouted, "Chad!" She motioned her boyfriend to come to her then said to Kim, "Our turn."

An impromptu line formed behind Kim. All the couples wanted to have their picture taken in front of the magnificent Christmas tree and under the imaginary Mistletoe. Cody moved to the side and watched Kim. He tried to understand his feelings. When he was with Kim all he thought about was her. She made him feel so alive.

As if feeling his eyes, Kim turned. She scrunched her shoulders conveying 'what can I do?'

Cody smiled and mouthed, "It's OK."

When Kim turned away, Cody wandered to the buffet table in the center of the rec room. He was going to wait for Kim to eat with him, but he couldn't resist the homemade chocolate chip cookies. Music over the speakers stopped and in the gap between songs he heard shouts from the back of the room. Some of his friends, guys without dates, were playing video games. He snatched a couple more cookies and walked back to say hi.

Teenagers stood behind the couch and blocked his view. As he got closer, the Christmas music faded, overwhelmed by the rattle of machine guns and exploding bombs. He looked at the end of the couch almost expecting to see Boomer sitting there.

Imaginary soldiers from Call of Duty filled the 50-inch TV. There was a bright flash and a tank exploded. A soldier jumped out of the tank engulfed in flames. The players howled with laugher. Cody stood transfixed.

Then everything hit at once.

He screamed, "It's not a game!"

Startled, the teenagers fell silent. Amid the screech of bombs, Cody screamed, "Don't you understand it's not a game!"

Someone hit the pause button. The screen froze. The entire room fell silent.

His face filled with anguish, Cody said, "You don't understand what it is really like."

Kim ran across the room to him. She didn't know what to do. Everyone was staring at them. She took his arm, led him to the restroom and shut the door.

Cody grabbed the sink and started shaking uncontrollably. Images of his brother past and present came together. Everything he tried to hold inside suddenly burst. Sobs racked his chest.

Kim pulled him from the sink and squeezed her arms around him. She held him as tight as she could while he sobbed.

CHAPTER 32

Days passed. With the spring thaw, banks of fog cloaked the fields and forest. The river swelled from the run-off of melting snow and Grand Rapids held its collective breath. The river crested, then slowly receded and Grand Rapids sighed in relief.

Spring break came and the Walleyes returned to the river to spawn. Cody parked Boomer's truck on the bluff above the torrent rapids. Wearing his waders and carrying his fishing gear, he slowly made his way down to the water.

He pictured Boomer hip deep in the river casting his line, then beaming as he wheeled in a keeper. The sun slid behind a cloud and the image faded, replaced with an image of his brother in the hospital room.

He didn't know why he was drawn to the river. He stayed close to the bank and cast his lure into the tumultuous current. Almost immediately he had a strike that bent his pole as he hooked a fish.

He could almost hear Boomer excitedly shout, "Whoa! What'd you got there, Little Bro?"

He fought then spun in a 21 incher and tossed it up on the bank. The sun peeked through the clouds and reflected off the shinning iridescent Walleye.

Cody stared at the fish and suddenly knew what he needed to do.

On the way home Cody called Kim on her cell phone and when she answered he asked, "Do you want to go for a ride?"

"OK."

"Don't you want to know where we're going?"

"I like surprises."

"I need you to help me with the driving."

Joking, Kim said, "You mean I get to drive the truck?"

"I figured we could tie blocks to the bottom of your shoes."

Kim laughed.

"I…" Cody stammered suddenly not sure how she was going to respond. "I want to go see Boomer."

There was a long pause and Cody pictured Kim's forehead scrunched in thought.

"We can do that."

"Do you need to check with your grandparents?"

Another pause and Cody pictured Kim twirling her hair around her finger.

"It'll be OK."

"You sure?"

"Yeah." Kim's voice brightened. "When do you want to go?"

"Today."

Taken by surprise, Kim screeched, "Like today, today?"

"Yeah."

She drew in a breath her mind spinning, "When today?"

"Couple hours. I need to go home and pack a few things and clean the fish."

"Clean the fish?"

"I'll tell you all about it on the ride down."

Cody pulled into the open spot in front of the Photo Shop. He got out, then jumped up into the truck's bed. He glanced around to see if anyone was watching, then lifted the lid of one of the two strapped-down ice chests. On top of the ice was a Walleye wrapped in freezer paper. The rest of the gutted and cleaned fish were buried in ice. He took the wrapped fish and jumped down from the truck, then carried it into the shop.

Stanley came out from the back room when the bells above the door jingled. Cody walked up the aisle then set the package on the counter.

Mr. Lewinski adjusted his eyeglasses and asked, "What's this?"

"Walleye, fresh from the river."

"Are they running?"

Cody arched his eyebrows, "Oh, Yeah."

"How many you catch?"

"Mmm…"He rubbed his lower lip debating whether he should tell the truth. "They're … for Boomer."

Stanley raised his hand. "Don't tell me."

Raised arguing voices came from upstairs. A door slammed. Kim barged down the steps. She came into the room with an overnight bag on her shoulder, a pillow clutched to her stomach, and her face bright red.

Stanley took in the pillow then stared at his granddaughter.

"Not you, too." Kim flashed a petulant pout. "We're just going to see Boomer."

Cody tried to intercede. "We're going to stay with my mom."

Stanley said, "It's a long drive."

Kim snapped, "That why I'm going with him."

Stanley's eyes went from Kim to Cody then back to his granddaughter. His features slowly acquiesced.

"Do you have your cell phone?"

Kim tapped her overnight bag. Tension fled her face, replaced with the excited blush of adventure as she realized her grandfather was going to let her go.

Stanley went to the cash draw and took out some money. "Here." He held it out for Kim.

"I have money, Mr. Lewinski," said Cody.

Stanley put the money in Kim's hand then wrapped both his hands around her hand. Their eyes met and a fleeting look of loss and parting passed between them. Stanley slowly, reluctantly let his grown-up granddaughter's hand slip away.

Kim brightened and asked, "Will you take our picture?"

She took her camera from her overnight bag and gave it to her grandfather, then swung the bag up on her shoulder. She took Cody's hand and led him out to Boomer's truck. Outside the shop she said, "Wait," then set the bag on the sidewalk. She reached into the bag then brushed her hair back and put on a baseball cap. She smiled at Cody and quipped, "Got to look like a trucker." She climbed up the bumper and sat on the hood. Cody stood next to her, folded his arms across his chest, and leaned back on the red truck.

Stanley framed the shot: Kim wearing sneakers, jeans, a purple sweatshirt and a Mud Hens baseball cap, Cody in running shoes, jeans and a long-sleeve grey flannel shirt, their faces smiling, confident and filled with untold promises.

CHAPTER 33

For Cody the drive to Texas was so different with Kim. On the last trip, when he drove down with his dad, they hardly talked. Now, it didn't matter if he was driving or if Kim was driving they kept talking the whole time. As the mile markers sped by, Kim jumped from one subject to another with no rhyme or reason. One minute she would be talking about school, then her favorite books, movies she wanted to see, CD's she'd listen to as she fell asleep and food to die for which led them to get off at the next exit and pull into an all-night diner at three in the morning.

The parking lot was half full. Inside the small white rectangular diner most of the round stools along the counter were already taken. The patrons were a mixture of truckers, insomniacs, drinkers chased out when the bars closed, and woebegone nighttime travelers.

They sat by the window in a red vinyl booth where Cody could keep an eye on Boomer's truck and the prized fish in the ice chests. He didn't sit next to Kim, but across the table so he could look at her. Still wearing the baseball cap, Kim pushed her hair behind her ears as she studied the menu.

Kim said, "My stomach doesn't know if it wants dinner or breakfast. What are you going to have?"

Cody didn't even bother to open the menu. "Breakfast, bacon and eggs, hash browns."

"Bacon sounds good ... I think," She traced her finger down the menu, "I am going to have French toast smothered in warm syrup."

After the waitress took their order, Kim glanced around the diner full of late night characters, then leaned close to Cody and whispered, "Who are these people?" She started giggling and couldn't stop.

Cody tried to keep a straight face but lost it. He bit his lower lip to keep from laughing out loud. Diners at the counter turned in their seats to see what was so funny. Cody brought his finger to his lips and tried to say "shhh," but it came out as a whistle that only made Kim giggle harder. He knew part of the giggles was because they were up all night, but a big part was just Kim. She was happy by nature and her giddiness was contagious.

Kim's eyes swept the room, then she said in a conspiring whisper, "Maybe they only let them out to eat," which set off another round of the giggles.

The waitress set the food on the table: golden French toast with melting butter, bacon thick and crisp, eggs sunny side up with steaming hash browns.

Halfway through her breakfast, Kim paused with a fork-ful of French toast almost to her mouth. "Where are we?" She laughed and set the fork on her plate. "For the first time in my life, I have no idea where I am. Do you know where we are?"

Cody shook his head.

"This is so strange." She swirled the French toast in syrup then popped it in her mouth. She chewed and swallowed then said, "Last night I was in Grand Rapids sleeping in my own bed and now I'm a zillion miles away."

"Not a zillion."

Kim cocked her head to the counter and smiled. "Are you sure?"

Cody wondered if Kim had finally fallen asleep. Her head was resting on her pillow propped against the center console. She had kicked her shoes off, curled her feet on the seat and snuggled under her jacket. When they passed under the overhead lights near the freeway exit he checked on her but couldn't see her face. He gently brushed her hair.

Kim took his hand and held it next to her cheek. "Do you ever wonder why things happen? If my grandfather hadn't gone to Vietnam he never would have met my grandmother and brought her home to Grand Rapids. I wouldn't be here with you right now." She gave a sigh mixed with a yawn, then squeezed his hand. "I like being with you."

Cody felt Kim's soft breath on his fingers as she drifted into sleep. He was afraid to move, afraid that he would wake her. He wanted this feeling to last as long as the endless highway.

CHAPTER 34

Cody wanted it to be a surprise. He told his father he was going to Texas, but he asked him not to tell his mother and brother. As he turned into the Brooke Army Medical Center's parking lot he had second thoughts. His stomach tightened and his hands became clammy. And then there was Kim. Back home all he thought about was the trip down to Texas with her, but now that they were here what were they going to do? Did Kim want to see Boomer, but more importantly, did his brother want to see her.

"When I was a kid my grandfather would say, 'a penny for your thoughts,'" said Kim.

Cody put the truck in park and turned off the engine. He didn't know what to say. As he leaned against the steering wheel to stare up at the medical center, he felt a slight jab against his thigh. He stretched back and shoved his hand in his pocket. Pulling out his hand, he opened his clenched fist. The arrowhead brought back memories of the day he and his brother found the two arrowheads fused together.

Kim said, "What did Boomer call it ... a talisman?"

"Yeah." Cody closed his hand and slid the arrowhead back in his pocket. He head motioned to the burn unit. "Are you OK with this?"

Kim met his gaze and nodded. They got out of Boomer's truck and hand in hand walked up to the burn unit.

Cody couldn't help it. As he walked to the burn unit he felt like he was on a roller coaster slowly climbing a steep incline. When he walked through the doorway, the roller coaster plunged. He tried to force his stomach back down from his throat.

He knew his brother was no longer in intensive care. They stopped at the reception desk and got Private Brennan's new room number, then started down the hallway.

It took a few seconds for the receptionist to make the connection. She called after them, "Boomer."

Cody stopped and turned back.

The receptionist said, "We all call him Boomer." She glanced at the clock on the wall behind her desk. "He won't be in his room. He'll be down in the physical therapy."

"For how long?" asked Cody.

"The sessions should be just about done, but Boomer usually stays down there and works out."

Cody's shoulders sagged with tiredness and disappointment.

"You don't have to wait. You can go see him in the therapy room. Here." The receptionist took a pre-printed diagram of the hospital from the drawer. With a marker she traced the way to Boomer.

Cody held the diagram with both hands and followed it like a divining rod. Kim walked by his side. They took the stairs instead of the elevator to the second floor. The therapy room was at the end of the hallway. Cody stopped and neatly folded the map, then slid it into his back pocket. His heart was racing.

Kim took his hands and gently squeezed. He took a few shallow breaths then nodded that he was OK.

A metallic clank, clank, clank came from the therapy room. Cody entered the room filled with whirlpool baths and massage tables. A soldier dressed in fatigues was sitting on one of the exercise machines in the back of the room grunting as he did leg presses. His back was to them but Cody knew that grunt.

There was a loud clank as Boomer relaxed and the weights fell. He pivoted in the seat then hunched over to catch his breath while resting his arms on his knees. His hands and forearms were covered by grey burn gloves. The fingertips were open. The left glove was cut and modified to only cover his remaining thumb and index finger.

Cody quietly walked across the room.

Feeling his presence, Boomer looked up. He shouted, "Little Bro." He jumped up and wrapped his brother in a bear hug using only his upper arms leaving his forearms and hands extended behind Cody.

Cody said, "You're squishing me!"

He stepped back willed a smile to his face and kept it there. Boomer had changed. He was still hairless except for his eyebrows. His face was a blotchy mix of pinks and browns with transplanted skin tight across his chin and cheek bones making his prostheses nose seem out of place. Scars outlined the skin grafts on his neck.

What was most disconcerting for Cody were his brother's eyes. Healthy and undamaged, they were so out of place amid the scars on Boomer's face. He remembered when Captain Driscoll called them raccoon eyes. They were alive and mischievous and when Cody looked at them he saw his brother the way he used to be.

"Where's Dad?" Boomer asked.

"He's home."

"You drove all the way by yourself?"

"Nah, I had help."

Kim stood by the doorway. Cody waved her forward. As she crossed the room, he kept looking from Kim to Boomer.

Boomer recognized Kim. His panic filled voice said, "What's she doing here?" He spun so she couldn't see his face.

Cody didn't know what to do. Kim stopped next to him. They were like three statues in the room.

Kim moved forward. She stepped around and in front of Boomer. She looked up at his face and said, "Hi, Boomer."

Cody couldn't see his brother's reaction. The only change he saw on Kim's face was a hint of compassion behind her smile. If it would have been anyone else he didn't know what Boomer would have done. Boomer's shoulders' relaxed as he lowered his head to her.

"Hey, Kim."

CHAPTER 35

Boomer sat outside on the patio under a large umbrella wearing his army cap and sunglasses. Kim sat next to him talking non-stop filling him in on all the latest 'goings-on' in high school.

Cody struggled down the sidewalk with the ice chest bouncing off his hip. He plopped the chest down next to his brother.

"What do ya got?" Boomer asked.

Cody did a double take because he still couldn't pair the voice with his brother. Boomer's skin graft lips were still tight and swollen so when he spoke his lips hardly moved. The speech patterns were the same, but the words sounded strange because they came from his tongue, not his lips.

Cody opened the lid then slid his hands into the partially melted ice and lifted out a Walleye.

Boomer exclaimed, "Whoa!"

"Guess what's for dinner?"

His eyes like saucers, Boomer peered into the ice chest.

Cody lifted more Walleyes to the top. "Got another chest too."

"How many did you catch?"

"'bout 24."

"The limit's six."

"Right. Six for me, six for you, six for Kim and six for Mom." His eyes questioning he asked, "Where is Mom?"

Boomer turned serious. "You've got to help me, Little Bro. She is driving me crazy. You've got to help me convince her to go home." Boomer lifted his gloves and cradled his deformed hand. "I can take care of myself."

Cody asked again, "Where is she?"

Boomer sat back in his chair and shook his head. "They all love her around here. They think she's a saint. She meets with the families when they bring in a new crispy critter."

Cody's mouth dropped. He couldn't believe what his brother just said.

"What?" Boomer dismissed his brother's look. "That's what we are, crispy critters." He lowered his hands to his lap. "Anyways, Mom talks with the families ... lets them know what to expect..." His voice trailed off and he seemed to go into his own private place.

Cody and Kim stayed quiet.

Cody lowered the lid to the ice chest and that seemed to bring Boomer back.

"Kim, you like Walleyes?" asked Boomer.

"Sure do."

"But, do you know how to cook them?"

Boomer decided they weren't going to freeze any Walleyes. They were going to cook them all. He commandeered stoves in the hospital's kitchen and before long the tantalizing aroma of fried fish permeated the ward.

Boomer supervised while Cody fried the fish and Kim cooked a big pot of rice. When they were finished, Cody and Kim carried platters of food into the family lounge. Boomer went to gather his friends.

The lounge soon filled with nurses, doctors and then recovering burn victims. As devastating as Boomer's burns were, some of the soldiers' injuries were much more traumatic. Besides horrific burns many of the young soldiers had lost legs or arms from IEDs.

It was hard for Cody to look at them, not because of the scars and disfigurements, but because of the pain they suffered and continued to endure.

Around each other and the hospital staff the soldiers weren't self-conscious. As they ate and talked, Cody felt like an outsider. There was a bond between the soldiers and the medical personal that he was not and never would be a part of. What Cody found hard to believe was the way they laughed and joked with each other. They'd make fun of each others injuries. It was a black humor that they shared among themselves. Cody knew where Boomer got 'crispy critters'.

Boomer fed himself. His gloved hands looked like two bear claws wrapped around the knife and fork as he devoured Walleyes and scooped in rice. Cody wished he would have brought more fish. Boomer stopped with the fork halfway to his mouth. Cody followed his gaze to the door.

At first glance Cody thought it was a female nurse and then his face lit up. Without thinking he stood. His mother's eyes traveled from one son to the other.

"Cody."

Cody crossed the room. Eileen lifted her hand to his cheek as if checking to see if he was real. She wrapped him in her arms.

Cody led her to his place at the table as paused conversations and eating resumed. Not sure what to do, Kim slowly stood.

If Eileen was surprised she masked it well. She seemed truly happy to see Kim. She gently set her hand on Kim's shoulder and eased her back to her seat. Cody went and got a plate of food for his mother.

Eileen wore a simple white dress. Her hair was tied up in a bun. She wore no makeup and her only jewelry was her wedding band. Cody didn't remember his mother being so thin and pale as if she never saw the sun. To him she looked tired, especially her eyes.

Cody set the food in front of his mother then sat by a soldier who was in a wheelchair. Andy had two stumps beneath his hips and burns covered one side of his face. Cody looked around the room of caretakers and disfigured patients. Everything was so surreal, for him to be so healthy sitting next to Andy and for Kim to be so beautiful sitting by Boomer.

CHAPTER 36

It wasn't like the loaves and fishes and way too soon the last of the Walleyes disappeared. Cody and Kim carried the plates to the kitchen as the staff made their way back to their stations and the soldiers back to their rooms.

Looking pensive, Kim set the plates in the sink.

Cody asked, "Are you OK?"

"I'm fine."

"You were quiet during dinner. That's not like you."

Kim tried to smile, but failed. "It's hard."

Cody set his plates on top of Kim's then gathered her in his arms.

Kim said, "I never thought it would be this hard. It's one thing to look at photos…"

"I know."

"I'm tired. You've got to be exhausted. You did most of the driving."

Cody gave an acknowledging sigh then released her and led her back to the lounge.

Eileen stayed in the motel next to the Medical Center. Cody went to the truck and got their bags while Eileen took Kim and Boomer to her room. Cody figured they'd stay with his

Mom, but he never thought about where they would sleep. He carried the bags into the room and looked around not sure where to set them.

"Little Bro, you can bunk with me," said Boomer.

Cody gave his brother a quizzical glance.

"We can wheel another bed into my room. It's no big deal."

Cody looked at Kim who nodded her OK.

Boomer took Cody with him on his nightly rounds. Each evening he would stop and visit every soldier on his ward. Some of the soldiers he would just pop his head in and say goodnight, others he would spend time with checking to see if they needed anything or if there was anything he could do for them.

On the first couple stops, Cody felt awkward. He didn't know where to look. He was afraid if he stared they'd be upset and if he didn't look at them they'd be upset. When they'd joked he didn't know how to respond. It was OK for soldiers and Boomer to make fun of their injuries, but he didn't want them to think he would ever laugh at them.

So he followed Boomer's lead. He looked where Boomer looked and laughed when he laughed, and gradually he relaxed.

He was embarrassed when his brother introduced him as the stud quarterback. He knew Boomer was kidding but also proud at the same time. He was always amazed at the way his brother related with people. Boomer could talk with anyone and within minutes they'd be friends.

Andy had the room next to Boomer's and he was their last stop for the night. He was already in bed watching American Idol on the TV mounted on the wall.

"Check this out. This dude croaks like a frog," Andy said.

They watched the show for a while. Cody sat in a chair while Boomer sat in the empty space where Andy's legs should have been at the end of the bed. The next contestant was a cute blonde girl who sang a haunting Country-Western song. Watching Boomer and Andy stare at the screen Cody wondered what they were thinking.

When the song ended, Boomer said, "She ain't bad."

"I've had better," said Andy.

Boomer laughed. "In your dreams."

The extra bed had been wheeled into Boomer's room. Cody lay next to his brother. It felt almost like a camp-out except instead of stars they had the glow of lights in the parking lot outside of Boomer's window.

Boomer said in a subdued voice Cody hardly ever heard from his brother, "When they transferred me out of intensive care to this ward, I was really down, feeling sorry for myself. I pretty much stayed in my room the whole time. Jake McCloskey stopped in. God was he a sight. You think I'm bad? You should see him. We got to talking then he asked me to take the tour with him to meet the other guys. I was so embarrassed. Here I was feeling sorry for myself when these guys..." Boomer took a deep breath. "There was a Marine sergeant who was thrown from his Humvee when a roadside bomb detonated. Over 97% of his body was burned. He was here for 17 months and had over 100 surgeries. He learned to live with unbearable pain and I was feeling sorry for myself, right? When Jake left I took over doing the tours. It makes me realize how lucky I am."

They fell silent for a while, then Cody asked the question that was in the back of his mind on the drive from Grand Rapids.

"When are you coming home?"

Boomer didn't answer. Cody turned on his bed so he could see his brother. Boomer's head was propped up on pillows the light reflecting his rippled scarred face. He held his hands up with his elbows resting on the bed. Cody wondered if that was the way he slept. Were his hands too painful to rest on the bed and did he have to keep his head immobile all night?

Boomer said from the shadows, "There are no mirrors in here. You spend your time looking at other guys wondering how bad you look. Sooner or later you've just got to know. The first time I saw my new self was in the visitors' restroom." He touched his face. "I'm looking at the face in the mirror and saying it's not me. It can't be me. I'm not that freak in the mirror." Boomer covered his face with his hands. "How can I go home? Everyone would stare at the freak I've become. I want people to remember the way I was, not the way I am."

Cody didn't know what to say. He searched for answers but he couldn't find any. They both fell silent. Exhaustion overtook Cody and he started to drift off to sleep.

A soft whimpering came from Andy's room. Boomer got out of bed and went to him. Cody heard his brother's voice but not the words he said to Andy as sleep overtook him.

CHAPTER 37

In the morning when his mother and Kim weren't in their room, Cody quickly realized where they would be. The hospital chapel was non-denominational and open to everyone. An informal prayer service was held every morning. Sometimes ministers from different faiths would lead the service, other times hospital personnel. The wounded, family members and friends were invited to stand and share their favorite prayers.

Cody quietly entered the small Chapel. Most of the padded wooden seats were taken, so he stood along the back wall. Eileen and Kim were sitting in the first row. His mother was holding a young woman's hand. He recognized the girl from a photo on the nightstand in one of the rooms he and Boomer had visited last night. She was pretty in a plain and simple way and about his age. His mother stood and the girl stood with her. It was obvious the young woman was soon to bring a child into the world.

Eileen said the prayer in what Cody always felt was her church voice, a voice pure and strong that seemed to come from a special place within his mother.

Lord, make me an instrument of Thy peace,
Where there is hatred let me sow love,
Where there is injury, pardon,
Where there is doubt, faith,

Where there is despair, hope,
Where there is darkness, light,
And where there is sadness, joy.

Cody remembered lying in bed when he was a child. His mother would come to tuck him in and together they would say the Prayer of St. Francis. He whispered the words as his mother continued.

O divine Master,
Grant that I may not so much seek to be consoled as to console,
To be understood as to understand,
To be loved, as to love,
For it is in giving that we receive,
It is in pardoning that we are pardoned,
And it is in dying that we are born to Eternal Life.

Cody carried his bag down to the truck. Boomer walked next to him dressed in his army fatigues, cap and wrap-around sun glasses. Spring came much earlier to Texas than it did back home. Cody was wearing jeans and a t-shirt. Looking at the truck, he knew he should have stopped and washed it, but he was so excited to see his brother and give him the Walleyes that he didn't even think about it and now it was too late. The windshield and front grill were covered with smashed bugs and road grit hid the gleaming red finish.

He stammered, "I meant to wash…"

Boomer raised his hand telling Cody to stop. He walked up to his truck. He took off his right glove then glided his fingertips along the hood. His forearm was scarred. Disfigured tendons and misshaped fingers gave his hand a claw like appearance.

Cody asked, "Want to drive?"

"Nah." Boomer slipped his glove back on as he walked around the truck.

The more Boomer stared the more mortified Cody became.

"I'm going to wash and wax her soon as I get home."

"It's OK. It's just a truck."

Eileen and Kim walked across the parking lot. Kim was wearing her baseball cap with her overnight bag slung on the shoulder and her camera in her hand. She stopped and turned around and snapped pictures of the medical center then slowly, hesitantly approached the two brothers.

Boomer saw the camera and backed away. Kim kept moving forward her lips tight with determination. She knew what she wanted, but wasn't sure how to get it. She swung her bag off her shoulder and thrust it to Cody. As Cody put it in the truck she moved closer to Boomer.

"I want to take your picture."

Boomer shook his head. "No!"

Kim inched closer.

Boomer raised his hands. "No!"

Kim looked to Cody and Eileen for help, but neither one responded.

"Please, Boomer."

His voice mixed with anger and wounded pride, Boomer asked, "Why?"

"Because a picture captures a moment in time, good or bad, and some day you'll look back at the picture and remember being here right now." Kim glanced at Cody and his mother. "We'll all remember."

CHAPTER 38

Toward the end of May, Cody, like everyone else, was going stir crazy counting the days to summer vacation. As he walked to Boomer's truck, he inhaled the warm scent of freshly cut grass from the football and soccer fields. But this year was different, he approached summer break with mixed emotions. His Dad was swamped. He was remodeling four houses, running from one work site to another. Cody knew his father needed his help and his summer would be filled with 12-hour workdays. In some ways he looked forward to being back on the job. He could feel the hammer in his hand and the sun on his back, but since returning from Texas something changed inside him.

Boomer had wanted to join the army. He had wanted to be a warrior to protect his village. He could still see his brother standing atop Buffalo Rock with his arms stretched to the sky. As a warrior he was tragically injured and will carry his scars and disfigurements for the rest of his life, but through all his pain and suffering never once did he hear Boomer regret the choice that he made.

Cody was jealous of his brother because Boomer knew what he wanted to do with his life and then he did it. He found something that was worth his sacrifice.

Cody would spend the summer working with his father, but he knew that wasn't what he wanted to do for the rest of his life. He desperately wanted to find what Boomer discovered, something that would give his life meaning.

Driving down the driveway to his house, Cody stopped. He thought for a second his mind was playing tricks on him. He blinked, but the image of his mother working in her garden was still there. He parked next to the garage and ran to her.

Eileen stood with her hands covered in dirt. Her hair was pulled back in a ponytail under a straw hat. She wore jeans and a white flannel shirt with the sleeves rolled up above her elbows.

Exuberant, Cody asked "When'd ya get home."

"This morning, I took a cab from the airport."

"Why didn't you call me? I would have come and gotten you." Cody didn't wait for her answer. He looked to the house. "Did Boomer come with you?"

"No."

Cody's high spirits sank and he said with a touch of reproach, "I thought you and Boomer would come home together."

Eileen kneeled and pulled weeds from the flowerbed. "He doesn't want to come home."

Cody thought about the last night he spent with his brother in Texas and how Boomer was afraid everyone would stare at him like he was some kind of freak.

"Do you think he'll ever come home?"

"I hope so, but you know Boomer when he makes up his mind..."

Cody asked because he wanted to know to understand. "Why did you come home without him?"

Eileen rubbed the dirt from her fingers. "I did all I could. Now it's up to Boomer."

With his mother home, their life took on a semblance of normalcy that Cody missed. Curtains were pulled back, windows opened and flowers placed in vases on the tables and windowsills. More importantly for Cody, his mother and father went back to the way they were before Boomer's injuries. He knew there was a rift between his parents that involved Boomer. Somehow they were able to heal the wounds that separated them.

With his mother's return came the return of Sunday dinners. Eileen asked Cody if he wanted to invite Kim. When Kim asked what she should bring, Cody laughed knowing his mother was going all out. He said, "Just bring yourself."

Kim sat in Boomer's seat. Jack carved the roast as Cody filled his plate. It took all his willpower to keep from digging in until everyone was seated and they said grace. For her being so little, Cody couldn't believe how much Kim ate. She kept saying, "Eileen this is so good and I can't eat anymore." Then she would take another helping.

After dinner, Eileen carried in plates of hot apple pie with melting vanilla ice cream. She set a plate in front of Kim, whose eyes grew as she mouthed, "I can't." She played with her spoon then gave up and scooped a piece to her mouth.

When desserts were finished no one seemed to want to move. Jack and Eileen lingered over their coffee. Cody pushed back from the table, stretched his legs and rested his hands on his stomach. Kim rested her chin on her hands looking guilty and pleased at the same time.

Eileen got up from the table, walked to the mantelpiece above the fireplace and returned with a small box. She gave the box to Jack and said, "Boomer wanted me to bring this home."

Jack opened the box and stared. "Good Lord." He whispered solemnly, "The DSC." He set the box on the table for all to see. The bronze cross was two inches high and almost as wide with an eagle on the center. A scroll beneath the eagle bore the inscription 'For Valor'. Jack intoned, "The Distinguished Service Cross is the second highest honor a soldier can be accorded. It is awarded for extraordinary heroism that involved risk of life."

Cody lifted the medal from the box. He turned it over. The center of the cross was covered by a wreath engraved with his brother's name. "Did Boomer ever talk about it?"

"No," said Eileen.

Cody passed the medal to Kim then looked to his mother. "What happened to the third soldier? The one they brought back with Boomer."

Sorrow filled his mother's eyes. "He died two weeks ago."

Cody shook his head in disbelief. "They all died. Boomer …" He couldn't go on. He thought about his brother's injuries knowing those he tried to save were all dead.

CHAPTER 39

Cody tied a bandana around his forehead to try and keep the sweat from dripping into his eyes. The temperature was in the 90's but up on the roof it was well over 100 degrees. His hands were so wet and slick that he had to concentrate to keep the hammer from slipping through his fingers as he pounded shingles in place.

Jack pulled up in his SUV and watched his son on the roof. Cody nailed the last of the lot of shingles, then slid his hammer into his tool belt and climbed down the ladder to get more shingles, grateful to escape the scorching sun on the roof.

Jack tossed him a bottled water from the cooler in the SUV. "It's just too dang hot."

Cody chugged the water. He couldn't seem to drink it fast enough. When he finished his dad tossed him another bottle.

"Why don't you call it a day?" Jack said.

"It's not even noon."

"Yeah, I know, but it's going to get hotter."

Cody took his cap off and shook it spraying beads of water. He knew his father was right. His jeans were soaked and stuck to his legs. "I can work on the drywall in the kitchen."

"The electricity's off. It's not any cooler in the house."

"Practice starts in two weeks." Cody slipped off his bandana and wiped the sweat from his face, then put his cap back on. He studied the farmhouse he had been working on for the last month. "I want to finish before then."

"I'll send Scott and Tony over on Monday to help you."

Cody kept staring at the house thinking about all that needed to be done.

"It's Saturday. Take the afternoon off."

Cody shook his head.

"When I was your age on a day like this we'd head down to the quarry." Jack walked to his SUV and opened the door. He looked back. "Why don't you call Kim?"

Cody's face broke into a grin that matched his father's. He unbuckled his tool belt and swung it over his shoulder, then went to get his cell phone as his dad drove away.

The river was fine for fishing and canoeing, but for swimming on a hot summer day nothing could beat the quarry. From the air it looked like a mystical giant scooped out a shovel of earth, leaving behind towering walls of limestone. Salisbury Quarry was known for incredibly clear and incredibly cold water. From the cliffs you could watch scuba divers explore old cars and a small plane that were sunk in the deep end of the quarry. In the shallow end, swimmers swam on the sun-warmed surface, but only the hardiest dove beneath the top thermal layer.

Cody carried a small cooler in one hand and a blanket in the other down to the white pebbly beach.

Teenagers laying and sitting on towels and blankets lined the water's edge. Carp, the center from the football team, shouted from among the sun bathers, "Nice legs, Cody!"

Kim burst out laughing.

Working outdoors, Cody often didn't wear a shirt, but he always wore jeans. His face and upper body were bronzed from the sun, but his legs beneath his swimsuit were stark white.

Cody sent Carp a sharp cut-it-out glance, but that only made Carp laugh. Still laughing, Kim pulled Cody's arm and led him to an open spot by the water.

Cody shook out the blanket and spread it on top of the sand. Kim tossed down the two beach towels she was carrying, then slung the beach bag from her shoulder. She took off her white cover-up revealing a one piece black swim suit that matched her black floppy hat. Not using her hands, she gracefully sat down on the blanket, then searched in the bag for sun screen. Trying to hide his legs, Cody sat Indian style next to her.

Kim lathered her face, arms and legs, then handed the sun screen to Cody.

"Can you do my back?"

Cody squeezed some sun screen on his palm then rubbed his hand on the back of her shoulder.

Kim flinched and squeaked, "Ouch!"

"What?"

"Your hand's like sand paper." She grabbed his hand and looked at his palm. "You've got to use lotion, Cody." She scraped off the remaining sun tan lotion and spread it on his nose and cheeks. She reached into the bag for her body lotion and massaged the lotion into the cracks and crevices in his palm and on top of his calluses.

When she finished one hand, he gave her the other. He stared at her as she massaged his hand. She seemed so serious and intent. Feeling his stare, she lifted her eyes to his. Her face eased into a smile that stopped his breath.

CHAPTER 40

Lying on her stomach, her chin resting on her palms, and swinging her bare feet back and forth, Kim stared at the group of teenage girls sprawled on towels, their skin glistening with lotion in the late afternoon sun.

"I could never be a sun bunny."

Cody was lying on his back, resting, with his eyes closed. "What?" He rolled to his side and followed her gaze. He laughed. "Sun bunnies?"

She tugged her floppy hat lower on her forehead. "Seriously, I couldn't do it. How can anyone spend hours out here everyday doing nothing, but trying to get the perfect tan?"

Cody shrugged.

Kim shifted her gaze to the wooden raft supported by empty 50-gallon drums that was anchored in the middle of the quarry.

"Want to race?"

"What?"

She pointed to the floating raft. "How much of a head start do you want?"

Cody said with mock seriousness, "You're going to give me a head start."

"It's only fair."

Cody snorted a laugh. He rolled to his stomach, dug his toes into the sand then dashed to the water. Kim tossed her hat to the blanket and raced after him. Cody ran into the cold water, then dived. He was a power swimmer thrashing his arms while kicking his feet.

Kim was graceful as a dolphin. Her body slid effortlessly atop the surface. Her arms and feet moved with a matching rhythm. Halfway to the raft she swam by Cody, who was thrashing and churning water. She climbed the ladder to the raft, then lay down on her stomach and peered over the edge.

Cody grabbed the ladder, his chest expanding-contracting as he sucked air and looked for Kim. When he saw her atop the raft, he let go and fell back into the water. He treaded water until his breathing slowed then climbed up the ladder and sat next to her.

"I'm not having a good day. First everyone makes fun of my legs and now I get thoroughly thrashed by a girl."

"Poor baby."

Cody lay on his stomach resting his chin on his arms staring at the sun bunnies on the beach and teenagers playing volleyball in the sand court. His hair was sun streaked, his face tan, his eyes sparkling blue in the bright sunlight. He turned his head and looked at Kim.

Kim touched his cheek. She looked like she wanted to say something.

"What?"

She shook her head.

"What?"

"It's... the way you make me feel when you look at me."

"Cody!"

Cody sat up and turned. A path led down to a ridge in the limestone cliff. Carp and some of his football teammates were lined up on the promontory jutting out over the quarry getting ready to jump or dive into the clear water.

Carp waved his hands over his head making sure he had Cody's attention. He ran the few steps to the end and jumped. He pulled his knees to his chest and wrapped his arms around them as he cannonballed. A gigantic geyser of water splashed the cliff. Cody marked its highest point. Carp bobbed to the surface and treaded water as the other boys looked to Cody.

Cody shouted, "Not even close!"

Carp smacked his hand on the water then swam to the beach.

"What was that all about?" asked Kim.

Cody pointed, "See where the boys are."

She nodded.

Cody traced his finger along the cliff. "Now go straight down, see the rock that looks like a triangle."

Kim nodded again.

"That's Boomer's point. He did a cannonball that shot water all the way up to that spot. No one else has ever been able to come close."

Cody pictured his brother standing on the cliff. He saw him run and leap. He heard his 'war cry' all the way down to the water. When he rose and broke the surface and Cody pointed to the spot, his brother's boyish face became a mask of incredible triumph.

"I want him to come home," Cody said.

"I know."

CHAPTER 41

Cody parked in front of the Photo Shop. He finger-combed his hair in the mirror. When he got out of the truck, he winced as his foot touched the ground. He had sprained his ankle at football practice and it was still sore and slightly swollen. The over-the-door bells jingled as he entered the shop. Mr. Lewinski and Kim were talking behind the counter.

Stanley looked up and said, "Cody."

"How are you doing, Mr. Lewinski?"

"Busy, with fall classes starting up." He tossed his hands in the air then glanced at his granddaughter. "Luckily, I have Kim." He took off his glasses and wiped them with a cloth he used to clean camera lenses. "Any news on Boomer?"

Cody wondered if Boomer was what they were talking about.

"No."

Stanley slipped his glasses back on. "Do you know anything about the Guinea Pig Club?"

For a second Cody thought Mr. Lewinski was making a joke. He laughed.

"Is it like a Four H Club?"

"No, Not at all." Stanley finger-brushed his thick white mustache. "During World War II the Battle of Britain was fought in the air. The heroes were the fighter pilots. All across

England people would look up to the sky and see their modern day knights engaged in dogfights. During the course of the battle a number of planes were shot down. Some pilots parachuted to safety, some crash-landed. Aviation fuel is extremely flammable. When the planes were hit they would burst into flames. Many of the pilots who survived the crashes were horribly burned on their faces and hands. At the beginning of the Battle of Britain they didn't know how to treat devastating burns, so most of the airmen who survived the crashes ended up dying from shock, exposure and infection."

Stanley paused and checked to see if Cody and Kim were following the story.

"Sir Archibald McIndoe was a pioneer in plastic-reconstructive surgery. He knew in order to save these horrifically burned pilots from dying from exposure and infection they needed skin grafts. Working at Queen Victoria Hospital, he developed techniques that had never been used before. The pilots who came under his care became his guinea pigs. Pilots who had reconstructive surgery at Queen Victoria Hospital became members of the 'Guinea Pig Club.'"

Cody could easily picture Mr. Lewinski giving a lecture in a college classroom. He had the persona of a teacher. Cody thought the story was interesting, but he didn't know why Mr. Lewinski was telling it. He couldn't see what the Guinea Pig Club had to do with him.

"More and more pilots survived. Sir McIndoe was faced with a dilemma. What's to become of these badly burned, disfigured pilots? The policy at that time was to keep them separated from the public. Sir McIndoe was able to save these heroes from the Battle of Britain only to have them confined to a hospital."

Cody thought about Boomer and the other soldiers in the burn unit.

"Sir McIndoe realized saving their lives wasn't enough. He had to find a way to get them back into society. He left the hospital and went to the neighboring town of East Grinstead. He visited families, shops, pubs and told the citizens about the airmen under his care. He told them who they were and how they got their injuries and then he asked them to invite these men into their town."

Cody studied Mr. Lewinski knowing there was a purpose behind his story.

"The pilots came out of their rooms and went into the town. As one of them said, 'East Grinstead was the town that never stared.'"

CHAPTER 42

During the first game of the new season, Cody took a quick three- step drop back from his center while cocking the football. His receivers ran out patterns to the sidelines. Then, just like Coach Stutz predicted, he saw the opening in the center of the line next to Carp. He tucked the ball and ran the quarterback draw. When he hit the opening, his receivers turned into blockers. He sprinted 30 yards untouched to the end zone.

He tossed the ball to the referee thinking that was way too easy. The band broke into the Generals' fight song as he kneeled to hold the ball for the extra point. The kick was good. He jogged to the sideline feeling maybe this year would be different. He had never beaten the Panthers and that game was still weeks away. He knew Coach said, 'take it one game at a time,' but he couldn't help thinking ahead to the game that defined their season.

On the football field he felt different from last year and completely different from two years ago when he was the starting quarterback as a sophomore. Part of it was physical. He added height and weight, but though he was stronger, he wasn't any faster and not more elusive. Standing next to Coach Stutz and watching the defense, he realized the big change was the way he saw the field. As a sophomore, he was lucky if he could find one receiver coming off the line. Now it was like he could see three different receivers all at the same time.

The other big change was the speed of the game. When he was a sophomore the game seemed to go way too fast. He couldn't keep up with it. Now when he played, time slowed down. For the first time, he felt himself getting out ahead of the plays.

Last year, every team they played seemed to be able to run the ball against the Generals. So it was no big surprise when the Coach of the Fighting Irish decided to go for it on fourth down. The surprise came when the Sanchez twins sandwiched the running back. Jose hit him low as Miguel hit him high, stopping the running back in his tracks. Cody buckled his chin strap and ran onto the field. The Sanchez brothers were only sophomores and this was their first year playing varsity. They were both linebackers and when they hit they hit as one. Cody high-fived the twins as they ran to the sideline thinking, wow, if we can slow down the running game...

Cody dropped Kim off at home. Since her grandfather had classes on Saturday morning she needed to get up early to open the shop. He was too revved up to go home. He was still high with the adrenaline rush of winning their first game of the season. He knew there was no way he'd be able to sleep. He felt like driving to unwind. He drove the streets of Grand Rapids and then as if Boomer's truck had a mind of its own, he found himself overlooking Buffalo Rock.

He shut off the lights and got out of the truck, then waited as his eyes adjusted to the darkness. A crescent moon cast a soft glow on the rippling water. Carefully, he made his way down the embankment. He couldn't see the stepping stones, but he knew they were there. With a leap of faith, he jumped, then sprang from one stone to the next. He grabbed hold of the limestone formation and pulled himself to the top.

A slight breeze rustled leaves on trees lining the banks. Night air was going through the yearly transition of summer to fall. He held his breath and fell under the soothing spell of water rippling over rocks.

Time passed. He lifted a pebble and tossed it as far as he could into the river. He heard the plunk, but couldn't see the splash. He wondered if he woke the Walleyes sleeping on the river's bottom.

Cody took the arrowhead from his pocket. He knew Mr. Lewinski told him the story about Sir Archibald McIndoe for a reason. He knew Kim's grandfather was trying to give him a way to bring Boomer home, but he couldn't see it. He couldn't change his brother's scars or Boomer's mindset that everyone would look at him like he was a freak.

Frustrated, he went through the story again. What did the pilot mean when he said, 'The town that never stared'?

He squeezed his hand so tight that the arrowhead cut into his palm and as if sharing his brother's pain he realized, if he couldn't change Boomer, then he would have to change the town.

CHAPTER 43

On Sunday afternoon, Cody sprayed Boomer's truck with the garden hose, then took the soft, soapy rag from the bucket and tossed it on the hood. Kim pulled into the Brennans' driveway and parked behind the truck. She walked over, picked up the hose up and eyed Cody.

Watching Kim, Cody rubbed the rag in wide circles on the hood.

"Don't even think about it."

Her eyes full of happy mischief, Kim sucked on her lower lip. She shot a quick burst. Cody ducked behind the truck. As the water stopped, he peered over the edge. Kim fired again.

"Cut it out!" He tried to sound angry, but that only made her laugh.

Keeping the nozzle pointed at him, she walked over to her 10-year-old brown Honda Civic, then turned and sprayed her car. Still watching her, Cody went back to washing the truck. Kim dropped the hose, rolled up her sleeves, sashayed to the bucket and grabbed another rag then started washing her car.

When Kim finished, Cody was not even halfway done. She tossed the rag in the bucket then shook her hands air drying them while smiling like a perky model on a TV commercial. Teasing him, she swiveled her hips and pointed her fingers from the truck to her car.

"It's done in half the time and gets better gas mileage too."

Cody playfully threw the rag. She ducked under it and laughing, ran to the porch.

Kim came out of the Brennans' house carrying a paper plate of oatmeal raisin cookies.

She held the plate out like a peace offering. "Here."

Cody slid his hands under his armpits and dried them against his shirt. He snatched a cookie and popped it in his mouth.

"Gross."

"What? My hands are clean."

Kim rolled her eyes. She took a cookie and ate it with small bites. Between the two of them the cookies soon vanished.

Cody used a chamois cloth to buff dried wax on the hood of Boomer's truck. Kim stood across from him on a step stool buffing the other side.

Slowly, methodically while polishing the hood, Cody said, "I keep thinking about what your grandfather said ...about 'the town that never stared.'" He turned the cloth over to the clean side. "Boomer doesn't want to come home because he thinks everyone will stare at him like he's some sort of freak." He shook the cloth. "But that's what they're going to do if he comes home." He rubbed the cloth against the hood. "They're going to stare at him like he is a freak."

"Are you sure?"

"You've seen, Boomer."

"Do you think he's a freak?"

"No!"

"Why not?"

Cody opened his mouth but no words came out. He concentrated on buffing. His hand circled the hood as his mind circled the question.

"When I look at him I see my brother."

"I see my friend," said Kim

Frustrated, Cody tossed the cloth up in the air. As it fell back to the hood he asked, "So what do we do?"

"We have to find a way for people to see Boomer the way we do."

Cody stared at her across the hood. "And how do we do that?"

CHAPTER 44

Cody sat next to Kim in front of her computer in the Grand Rapids Photo Shop. The shop was closed for the day. Kim's grandmother was quietly cleaning cameras in the display case with a feather duster.

Kim clicked from one photo to another. "We need to create a montage."

The photos were all of Boomer, but they were not Brennan family pictures. They were photos Kim had taken through the years for the school paper and yearbook, some were published, some Cody had never seen before. As one photo after another appeared on the screen, Cody was flooded with memories. He watched his brother age before his eyes, but one feature never changed, Boomer's smile. No matter the background, Boomer always had the same slightly goofy smile as if life was a game and not meant to be taken too seriously.

Kim stopped at the photo of Cody and Boomer taken at last year's Panthers football game. The boys stood side by side staring into the camera with Cody in his football uniform holding his helmet and Boomer attired in his army dress uniform his beret cocked at a jaunty angle.

Kim took a deep breath and clicked to the next picture. Cody couldn't help it. He gasped. It was one of the pictures Kim had taken at the burn unit before they left Texas. Boomer had taken off his cap and sunglasses and she had taken a picture of his face.

Cody felt the light touch on his shoulder. He turned and looked at Ahne who stared at the photo. Her sigh was a mixture of pain and sadness. She whispered soft words in Vietnamese that neither he nor Kim understood. He wondered if it was a prayer. Ahne took her hand from his shoulder, then went upstairs.

Kim clicked to a photo of Boomer with his raccoon eyes above scarred cheeks and deformed lips.

"We need to prepare people so they won't be shocked when they see Boomer."

Cody was suddenly overwhelmed with a feeling of helplessness.

Cody sat silently watching Kim work. She selected 25 pictures of Boomer, cropped and edited the photos, then looped the pictures in a moving slide show. She had the uncanny ability to select photos that captured his brother's essence – everything that was good and right about him. Many times there were other students in the photos, but Boomer always seemed to be the center of attention not only because of his size, but also because of the forcefulness of his personality. He appeared larger than life. The first 23 pictures were of Boomer as a student and athlete, the 24th was of him standing at attention in his army dress uniform while they played the National Anthem at last year's Panthers game. Only the 25th - the last photo - showed him as he looked today.

Boomer's ravaged face stared at Cody from the screen.

Kim said, "You have to tell the story that goes with the pictures. Only you can do that."

CHAPTER 45

Cody stood with Chad by Coach Stutz among his teammates, his friends. The Generals bleachers were overflowing with students and town folks. The band was marching off the field after playing the Generals' fight song. It was a Friday night that was made for football with a slight chill in the air, not enough to make you cold, but enough to get the blood stirring. The stadium lights cast a glow that seemed to envelope the players and fans in a bond of camaraderie. Cody took off his helmet and turned to the bleachers seeking his mother and father. When he found them he waved his helmet.

Chad raced to the corner of the end zone. Cody lofted the ball over two defensive backs. Chad dragged his toes along the green turf while extending his hands as high as he could. The ball gracefully fell to his fingertips. He clutched the ball to his chest and still with his toes in bounds fell to the field.

Cody knew it was a picture-perfect play. He couldn't have thrown the ball any better and Chad couldn't have made a greater catch. Fans' cheers rang inside his helmet. It was only the fourth game of the season, but the team was playing at a higher level then they played at any time last year.

He and Chad were clicking. Their chemistry was the result of the countless hours spent running routes over the years. Timing was everything. Now, it was like they both had the same mental clock and vision of the plays. Cody would throw the ball to an empty spot on the field knowing Chad would soon be there to catch it.

Cody couldn't keep the ear-to-ear grin from his face as he went to the sideline. The game was fun again. After Boomer left, he took the game way too seriously and even when they won, he felt no joy.

When he went through the photos of Boomer with Kim, he found what was missing. In any photo he saw of Boomer playing football, his brother was always grinning. It didn't matter if they were winning or losing he was having fun. Somehow along the way, Cody forgot that football was just a game.

As his attitude changed so did the team's. Gone was the feeling of gloom and doom left over from last year's loss to the Panthers. Practices still were hard, but lighthearted. Pranks returned to the locker room, boisterous laughter echoed in the showers. On the field the team played loose and won.

Kim was waiting outside the locker room with her camera hanging from her neck. When Cody came out she dashed to him and said, "Look."

Her face beamed with a pleased-with-herself smile. She turned the camera so Cody could see the photo. She had caught Chad just as the football touched his fingertips.

"Wow! That's a great shot, Kim." He glanced back over his shoulder. "Don't let Chad see it or we'll never hear the end of it."

"You're not jealous, are you?"

"Of Chad. No way. He makes me look good."

Kim slipped her hand through his arm. They walked to the parking lot. The lights were still on over the football field.

Cody impetuously said, "Come on."

He led her into the stadium and up into the empty bleachers. He sat with his eyes moving like he was replaying the game. Kim clicked through the photos on her camera. She poked him in the ribs then raised her eyes and gave him her smile. Cody looked at the photo of the Sanchez twins on the camera. Somehow each boy managed to grab a different leg of the Knights running back as they pulled him to the turf. Cody chuckled and glanced back to the field.

She clicked the camera off then leaned against his shoulder. "What's it like out there?"

Cody said the first thing that came to mind. "It's fun."

Kim chortled, "Fun? You didn't look like you were having too good of a time when you were on the ground after the linebacker blitzed you."

Cody winced at the thought. "That part wasn't fun." His hand swept the field. "But when everything goes right, when you run the play just like we do in practice and it works, and if it's for a touchdown, the kick you get is amazing."

"And I suppose you don't even notice the cheerleaders going all gaga."

"Well..." He tried to suppress a smile.

Kim poised her hand as if she was going to smack him. He caught her small hand in his and pulled it to his lap then looked back to the field. She leaned against his side.

He grew silent and Kim could feel the missing presence. It was as if she knew his thoughts were drifting to his brother.

"I showed Boomer's slideshow to Mrs. Reid."

Cody continued to stare at the field.

"Then we went and showed them to Mrs. Solis."

He held his breath.

"Then we all went and showed them to Principal Schmincke."

Cody released his breath and her hand. He leaned forward, put his elbows on his knees and steepled his fingers by his mouth.

"Are we doing the right thing?"

"We want Boomer to come home."

Cody nodded. His eyes and lips tightened with determination.

"Principal Schmincke said we could do the slide presentation during the assembly on Friday."

Cody squeezed his hands into fists and blew into them trying to fight the rising panic in his chest.

Kim said, "We can do this."

CHAPTER 46

The gym was hot and stuffy packed tight with students sitting elbow to elbow for the all-school assembly. Freshmen, sophomores and juniors were in the bleachers. Seniors sat on folding chairs in front of the stage. Principal Schmincke was talking at the podium, but it was like he was on a different frequency that Cody couldn't pick up. Cody wiped his sweating hands against his thighs, then shoved them in his pockets. He tried to still his tapping feet. His mouth was so dry it hurt to swallow.

Sitting next to him in the first row, Kim touched his arm. Her face was flushed with fear and concern, but not for herself.

"You're white as a sheet."

He wet his lips and hoarsely mumbled, "I'm OK."

He heard Principal Schmincke say Boomer's name and then his own. He stood and the room started spinning. He would have stumbled if Kim hadn't stood and grabbed his arm.

Students cheered and the gym took on the air of a pep rally. He regained his balance and walked unsteadily to the stage with Kim hovering by his side. As he mounted the steps and walked to the podium the cheers rose to a crescendo.

Kim went and sat by the projector with her eyes nervously dancing from Cody to the students.

Cody held onto the podium and smiled weakly to his audience, which only made the crowd cheer louder. Gradually the cheers subsided until the only sound was the rustling of chairs on the wooden floor.

Cody said, "I..." his voice broke and he couldn't go on.

In the silent gym with every eye upon him, he stood paralyzed. Time froze.

Kim pressed the projector's button and a larger than life image of Boomer filled the screen next to Cody.

Carp shouted, "Boomer!"

And like a chant the football team joined in. "Boomer! Boomer! Boomer!"

Cody turned and saw Boomer's senior yearbook's picture. Wearing his football jersey and crouched in a three-point stance, he looked like he was going to charge out of the screen and level any opponent in his way. The chant slowed and then stopped. The students' stares returned to Cody.

He swallowed and said, "I want to tell you about my brother."

Cody became a storyteller. With each new photo that flashed on the screen he spun a vignette of his brother's life. Many of his friends and older students relived the moments where Boomer's life force crossed theirs. Cody found himself laughing with them as he relived some of his brother's famous escapades. The freshmen and sophomores who didn't know Boomer were aware of him, a whispered legend who lingered in the halls and locker rooms. He now came to life.

The atmosphere changed when the photo of Boomer, in his Army dress uniform standing at attention as they played the National Anthem during last year's game against the Panthers, appeared on the screen. Gone was the lightheartedness and laughter. The room grew quiet almost somber.

Cody stared at his brother's image trying to draw on his strength.

"As many of you know, Boomer was injured in Iraq. He was hurt when he tried to rescue his teammates. Their Humvee was hit by an IED and exploded in flames. Boomer fought his way into the wreckage and somehow managed to bring out three soldiers."

Cody stopped and looked back to the photo.

"While trying to save their lives, Boomer was burned." Cody stopped and clutched the podium. "He's at the burn unit at the Brooke Army Medical Center in Texas. He's been there for months. The doctors are doing all that they can but..."

His fingers shook at he pointed to the screen. He looked to Kim wondering how he could go on. When their eyes met, he realized he wasn't alone. She was with him and so was his brother.

His voice broke on each word. "I want Boomer to come home." His eyes watered and he willed himself not to cry. "And I want you to see him the way that I do ... to see Boomer as our hero."

He looked to Kim and she clicked to Boomer's last picture.

CHAPTER 47

It was Carp's idea. On the following Monday in the cafeteria, he said it would be cool to take a picture of the football team and send it to Boomer letting him know he was in their thoughts. He figured they could do it after school before practice began when their uniforms were still somewhat clean.

Word quickly spread from student to student. Not just the football players, but all the students wanted to be part of the picture. When the final bell rang the buses remained empty. The student body gathered in the football stadium.

Kim set to work. Cody was amazed at the way she could be quiet, almost timid in the classroom, and then suddenly become a spinning gyro of energy taking complete control of a photo shoot. Diminutive and elfish, she either cajoled or intimidated the towering-over-her football players to stand where she wanted them, then had the students fill the bleachers behind the team.

The banner was Chad's idea. He made it in art class. After he put on his uniform, he carried the three-foot high roll out to the stadium. He had each football player hold the top of the sheet as he slowly unwound the paper roll that said in big black letters,

COME HOME BOOMER.

Cody and Kim sat at the dining room table in the Brennan's house. Beneath the table they entwined their fingers. Jack and Eileen sat with them, each reading a copy of the latest issue of the *Grand Rapids Gazette*. On the front page there were two photos of Boomer, one in his football uniform from the high school yearbook and the other, the photo Kim had taken of him outside the burn unit. Above the photos was the caption, 'The Town That Never Stared,' by Cody Brennan, photos by Kim Lewinski.

After his talk at the high school, Kim asked Cody to write the article so that the whole town would know Boomer's story. That night he sat at his computer and for once the words flowed as he retold the story. He brought the article to Kim at the photo shop and she selected the 12 photos that best matched his words. She added the photo she took of the football team and students at the stadium to the end of the article. When they finished, Kim showed the story to her grandfather who convinced the editor of the *Grand Rapids Gazette* to make 'The Town That Never Stared,' the lead story for the next issue.

Cody didn't know how his parents were going to react. He nervously watched his mother's eyes behind her reading glasses. She read the story much faster than her husband, then took off her glasses and dabbed the tears from her eyes. She waited as Jack finished the story.

Jack traced his fingers over the words, COME HOME BOOMER then folded the newspaper back to the front cover.

He said with a catch in his voice, "Excuse me."

He abruptly left the dining room and went out to the front porch. Eileen followed him. Cody went to join them, but Kim put her hand on his arm.

Cody could see his parents on the porch. His father stood with his back to them looking out to the yard trying to gather himself. Eileen walked forward and circled her arms around his waist and rested her head on his back.

Jack and Eileen came back to the dining room. Jack took his seat and set his hands on the *Grand Rapids Gazette*.

"Boomer needs to read this." He glanced at Kim. "To see this."

Cody said, "I could mail..."

Jack lifted his hand. "No, I need to..." He stopped and looked at his wife. "We need to be with him when he reads this."

Eileen nodded and set her hand on her husband's.

Cody said, "I'll go with you."

"No, you have school."

"But..."

"Cody," Jack's voice softened, "Son, this is something your mother and I need to do."

Chapter 48

Cody didn't know if it was worse being in school or at football practice during the week leading up to the game with the Panthers. In the hallways between classes all everyone was buzzing about was 'the game.' It wasn't bad enough that they were playing their archrival, but also for the first time in more then 20 years the Generals were going into the last game of their season undefeated. Students wore their school colors all week - some even bragged about wearing them to bed for good luck. Rumors circulated about a midnight raid to steal the Panthers' mascot. Cody tried to concentrate on his schoolwork amid the rising hype building into frenzy.

His parents were coming, but Boomer didn't know why. He was in the rehab room working out with the weight machine when one of the nurses gave him the message from his mother saying they would be there in the middle of the afternoon. He sat on the bench wondering what was up. His first thought was Cody. He pulled his dog tags out from under his shirt. In a clear plastic pouch hanging next to his tags was his arrowhead. Maybe his little brother got hurt at practice or…, but no, if it was something important like that, his mother would have stayed on the phone until they got him. He slipped his dog tags and arrowhead back beneath his shirt.

Boomer flexed his arms feeling a different burn, not the searing burn of fire but the burn of muscles trying to rebuild. From jogging and weight work, his legs were as strong as ever. Gradually he was regaining strength in his arms. He took off his gloves and flexed his hands. He knew they would never be like they used to be, but at least they were functional and for that he was deeply grateful.

He thought back to his last assessment with his doctors. They were very candid. He massaged the scarred palm below his missing fingers. Their words still rang in his ears, 'We have done all that we can.' He slapped the gloves against his thigh then headed to the showers.

In the family lounge of the Burn Unit at Brooke Army Medical Center, Boomer looked at the front page of the *Grand Rapids Gazette*. It took him a few moments to comprehend what he was seeing. He stood and screamed, "How could they do this!" He angrily swiped the paper from the table.

Jack said, "Boomer."

"They have no right!"

Eileen bent and picked up the *Grand Rapids Gazette*. She said in a stern voice that rocked him all the way back to his childhood, "Boomer, sit down."

Boomer sat and Eileen could see the pout behind his lips. She placed the newspaper in front of him.

"Read the story."

He heaved out a breath that sounded almost like a growl. Begrudgingly, he stared at the photos, and then placed his finger under the first line. As his finger moved, he mouthed the words.

Because of all his operations and scar tissue, Boomer's features seemed frozen. As he read the story, his face never changed only his eyes.

He finished the story and stared at the picture of the football team and the students in the bleachers and the banner that said, COME HOME BOOMER. He shook his head and his eyes filled with sadness.

"I can't go home."

Jack said, "Boomer."

He slowly lifted his disfigured face and looked at his father.

"If you can't go home, then how are the other soldiers here ever going to find their way home?"

Chapter 49

During football practice on Wednesday, Coach Stutz's whistle shrieked and the players froze. Coach waddled to the offensive line his rotund stomach bouncing with each thunderous step.

He screamed, "You've got to get lower." He lumbered down the line pushing each player's butt down. "Dig in!" He moved off to the side. "Again!"

Cody knew it wasn't just the players who were nervous and uptight. The pressure was getting to his Coach like everyone else. He moved back under center and called out the snap count. His junior tackle, Matthias, jumped early. Coach's whistle sounded like a scream. If it was a game they would have just gotten a five- yard penalty.

Coach looked like he was ready to pull someone's head off.

He shouted, "Take a water break!" then stormed off the field.

Carp glared at Matthias and snapped, "Get it right!"

The tackle's cleats clawed the field like he was trying to dig a hole in the turf to crawl into.

The trainer brought water to the field. Cody took his helmet off and sat on it. He took a bottle, squirted some water in his mouth, swished it, then spat to the ground. Carp and the rest of his teammates milled around not talking or even looking at each other. Cody shook his head in frustration. He wondered, what would Boomer do if he was here? What would he say?

He tossed the bottle back to the trainer, put his helmet on then went and picked up the football. Holding the ball, he windmilled his arm trying to keep it lose as he spun in a slow circle. He glanced at the deserted bleachers knowing on Friday night there wouldn't be an empty seat in the whole stadium. He stopped when he saw a solitary figure standing by the goalpost on the far side of the field. Even from 80 yards away, he could tell the person was large. There was something familiar about the way he stood. Cody squinted, but he couldn't bring the figure into focus. He took a step forward and then another feeling like he was in the river jumping from one stepping stone to another. And then he ran.

Cody pulled up a few feet from his brother. He took his helmet off and stood with his chest heaving not sure how to go on.

Boomer was wearing his army fatigues with his cap low on his forehead. He pushed the cap up and his eyes smiled.

"Little Bro."

Cody dropped his helmet and ran forward.

Boomer grabbed him. "Whoa!" He locked him in a bear hug and spun in a circle then released him and planted his hands on Cody's shoulder pads.

"Look at you. You're all grown up."

Cody laughed. "Am not."

Boomer pounded his brother's shoulder then pointed to the team across the field.

"What's going on out there? You guys look pathetic."

Cody looked at his Coach and teammates who were staring at them.

"Everyone is just wound way too tight."

"It's just a game."

"Try telling them that." He picked up his helmet. "Come on, I want you to meet some of the new guys. Maybe you can get them to unwind." He took a step toward his team.

Boomer hesitated.

Cody could feel the conflict raging inside his brother.

"They want to meet you."

Boomer jutted his jaw forward and as if following a decision he had already made, he shuffled ahead. Together the two brothers crossed the football field.

Cody thought there could not have been any better place for Boomer to start than with the football team. As he approached his teammates, he didn't watch his brother's reaction, but the players. He thought back to when Kim said, "We need to prepare people so that they won't be shocked when they see Boomer". He realized how tremendously important her words were. There were some looks of surprise at seeing Boomer at practice, but none of shock at the way he appeared.

Coach Stutz was the first to react. He revealed a side Cody had never seen of his coach before. Coach walked to Boomer and set his hands gently on his shoulders. The Coach's eyes watered as he said, "Welcome home."

Practice resumed. Boomer went from one group to another making corrections, offering words of encouragement, and just being Boomer.

The older players, the ones who knew him best, were the first to see the face beneath the scars and the rest soon followed.

CHAPTER 50

It was good to have Boomer in the locker room. Cody couldn't picture his brother up in the bleachers with his mother and father. Boomer was where he belonged. He felt his brother was as much a part of the team as he was. It was Coach's idea to have Boomer wear his old jersey and the team's to make him an honorary captain for tonight's game with the Panthers.

Cody was surprised with the effect his brother's presence had on the team. There were still nerves and jitters, but when Boomer walked among the players, his presence put the game in perspective. Looking at Boomer and the way his life had so drastically changed since high school made the team view the game in a whole new light. They wanted to win, but they also knew if they lost their lives would go on.

Boomer went from player to player with a word for everyone. Cody thought of his brother making his rounds in the burn unit and the soldiers who were still there.

Before they went out to the field, Coach Stutz asked Boomer to say a few words to the team. Reluctant to step into the spotlight, Boomer balked. Coach out-waited him. Boomer ponderously walked and stood next to the coach. He took his cap off and stared at Cody as if asking him to come up and take his place.

Boomer said, "Cody's the talker. He's the one who should be up here."

Cody shook his head.

Boomer bounced from foot to foot. He squeezed his cap between his gloved hands trying to find words that would have some meaning to the team.

"How you play the game tonight…one day you'll go back and relive it, but you can never go back and change it." He slid his cap back on, then walked and sat next to his brother.

The Generals charged out of the locker room leaving the two brothers alone. Cody tried to look at life through Boomer's eyes. He wondered how his brother felt knowing that all the students and practically the entire town of Grand Rapids were in the bleachers waiting for them. Was he scared?

Cody asked, "Are you OK?"

"No." Boomer shook his head as he looked through the open doorway to the stadium. The band broke into the Generals' fight song as the team ran onto the field. Boomer suddenly seemed dwarfed by the enormousness of the task before him. It was one thing to stand up in front of his friends, but another to meet the stares of the whole town. "If it was just me, I wouldn't do it." He slowly stood as if lifting an unbearable weight. "But it's like Dad said, 'If I can't do it, how can the others come home.'"

Cody saw the change come over his brother's scarred face and knew Boomer had made up his mind and nothing was going to stop him. His reconstructed lips turned up in a half smile and the glint returned to his raccoon eyes.

"I'll race you out there."

He ran.

Cody grabbed his helmet and ran after his brother.

Between the band playing and the students cheering it was beautiful chaos. Cody's heart was thumping his ribs as his teammates bounced off each other getting psyched.

The announcer called out the Panthers team captains. When he said each name, visiting fans howled out their Panthers cry. The captains stormed to the center of the field for the coin toss.

Not to be outdone, the home fans went wild as they introduced each of their captains. With clamorous cheers and pounding drums the captains stepped forward. The announcer paused and the stadium grew quiet.

In a sonorous tone echoing over the PA system, the announcer said, "Tonight's honorary team captain, Grand Rapids' native son, Private Boomer Brennan."

A hush descended over the field. It was almost like the stadium shifted as everyone leaned forward to see him.

His head up, his shoulders back, Boomer stepped forward. He took off his cap and held it by his heart. He stood under the harsh stadium lights his naked face exposed for all to see.

There were no gasps, no darting looks away, no eyes filled with pity. Someone in the bleachers clapped and like a pebble thrown into the river the sound rippled outwards and grew and grew into the most thunderous applause.

CHAPTER 51

Halftime ended and the Generals ran from the locker room back onto the field. Cody felt like he was living inside a dream. The first half seesawed back and forth and when the gun sounded the two teams were tied 24-24. The game was all that he expected and more. It was like there was magic in the air touching not only him but both teams and all the fans. Everyone he saw seemed to reflect his feeling that there was something special happening.

When he got onto the field he looked at his Mom and Dad and waved then searched...

"She's over there," said Boomer. He pointed to the cheerleaders.

Cody didn't see the cheerleaders only the girl taking their picture. "How'd you know..."

Coach screamed, "Cody!"

Cody backed away from his brother who shook his head with a tight grin.

After the second half kick-off, the Generals had the ball on their own 35-yard line. When Coach Stutz gave him the play, Cody's eyes sparkled.

He huddled the team not able to keep the smile from his face because he knew even before he called the play that it would work. The Generals weren't known for their running game. As Coach said, 'they'd only run the ball enough to keep the other side honest.' Most of the time Cody kept Tillman, his fullback, in as an extra blocker to pick up the blitz.

Cody set under center, checked his line and then Tillman behind him. He took the snap, back pedalled, then turned and stuck the ball into the running back's stomach. Tillman charged ahead. When the fullback hit the line he pivoted and tossed the ball back to the quarterback.

The defensive backs bit on the run. There was only a split second hesitation before they recovered, but that was all that Cody and Chad needed. Then it was like practice at a game. Cody's mental clock clicked down and when it hit zero he threw the ball. Not breaking stride, and as he had done thousands of times during practice, Chad cradled the falling ball to his chest, then ran to the end zone.

Adrenaline kept Cody going. He felt as psyched in the fourth quarter as he did at the start of the game. He felt like he could dink and dance forever, but it wasn't the same for the linemen. Massive bodies colliding play after play takes a mighty toll and even Carp was sucking wind as he struggled back to the huddle.

The Generals were down by three and had the ball at midfield close to their sideline. Cody dropped back to pass. Matthias completely missed his block. Cody saw the charging defensive end with the Panthers free safety right behind him. All he could do was hold onto the ball as the end smashed into him and threw him backward. In the heat of the moment, as

Cody struggled to get up, the free safety ran in and slammed him back to the turf.

It was the wrong thing to do.

A terrifying primal growl came from the sidelines. The small safety jumped up and sprang back. He took one look at Boomer charging at him then turned tail and ran as fast as he could back to the safety of his teammates.

Cody was more stunned than hurt. Boomer towered over him like a grizzly bear protecting his cub.

"You OK, Little Bro?"

"What are you doing out here?"

Cody got to his feet. He looked at his brother who stood glaring at the Panthers then to the safety who was cowering behind the large defensive guards. Seeing the safety shaking at the sight of Boomer, he couldn't help it, he laughed.

"Boomer!" He pushed his brother to the sideline. "Get out of here!"

The 15 yard penalty for the late hit on the quarterback moved the ball to the Panthers 35-yard line. With time ticking down, Coach Stutz pulled out all the stops and emptied his bag of tricks.

Cody called the play, set his team, took the snap then back pedaled. Instead of running downfield, Chad backed away from the line. Cody threw him a quick dart. Chad caught the ball and ran towards Cody's spot behind the center as the defense converged on him. Cody snuck through the line. Chad lopped a wobbling pass over the middle. With no one within 10 yards of him, Cody caught the pass and ran untouched to the end zone.

CHAPTER 52

It wasn't just Cody, but all eyes in the stadium kept shifting from the game clock to the field. No one could forget the Panthers stunning come-from-behind victory on the final play of last year's game. With 2:15 left to go, the Generals were up by four points. The Panthers had the ball on their own 40-yard line and had just used their last time out. Cody was going crazy. On the field he felt like he could control his destiny. On the sideline it rested in the hands of others. He realized you can try so hard, but there is only so much you can do by yourself. The rest is up to the team.

Three plays later, the Panthers were down on the Generals 25- yard line. There was just a little over a minute to go. A field goal wouldn't help the Panthers - they needed a touchdown to win the game.

The townfolk of Grand Rapids along with the entire student body were shouting, "DEFENSE! DEFENSE! DEFENSE!"

Cody took off his helmet. He wanted to pull his hair out. With each play the Panthers seemed to gain momentum. His biggest fear was that they would score and not leave the offense enough time to mount a comeback.

The Panthers' tailback broke through the line.

Cody and half the team screamed, "No!"

Jose Sanchez couldn't catch the runner. In desperation, he lunged at the Panther. With his body fully extended in the air, his hand clipped the runner's back heel. The back stumbled but managed to get his hand down to keep his knees from touching the ground. As he recovered and ran, Miguel, with a tremendous hit, smashed into his side. The ball popped loose. Jose scampered along the ground, grabbed the ball to his chest, and curled into a fetal position. The Panthers linemen piled on top of him trying to take the ball away, but there was no way Jose was going to give up the football.

The whistle blew. The referees tried to untangle the pile. Still curled on the ground, Jose wouldn't budge until his brother knelt down beside him. Miguel and Jose stood and raised the football in the air.

It was pandemonium on the Generals sideline and in the bleachers. With the ball lofted in the air, the Sanchez twins ran to the team. Cody and his teammates ran out and met them then engulfed the two boys.

There were still 26 seconds left on the clock. Coach Stutz sent his offense back on the field. Cody huddled the players by the 15-yard line. He looked back to the sideline. Jose walked up to Boomer and held out the ball. Boomer shook his head. Jose pushed the ball into Boomer's stomach.

Time slowed. Cody arranged the team in the victory formation. He took the snap, then took a knee. As time expired, he watched his brother standing tall between the Sanchez twins with the football clutched in his gloved hands.

CHAPTER 53

The Saturday after "The Game" as everyone was calling it, Boomer wanted to go in town to see if anything had changed while he was away. Cody tagged along thinking he'd have a chance to stop in and see Kim. Boomer drove. For Cody it felt good to sit up front with his brother - sort of like his world was getting back to the way it used to be.

The town was all decked out for Halloween. Cutouts of witches and scary cats were taped to store windows under brown and orange edgings. Kim was crouched down on the sidewalk trying to frame a shot of the pumpkins stacked up in front of the farmer's market. Boomer couldn't help himself. He coasted up behind her and blasted the horn. Kim practically jumped out of her skin, then spun around and glared.

Trying not to laugh, Cody opened the door and got out of the truck. He lifted his hands in a pacifying gesture.

"Don't look at me like that. I didn't do it."

Kim stomped forward and tapped on the glass.

Boomer powered the window down and sheepishly said, "Hey, Kim."

Kim tried to hold her glare, but couldn't. She tried to think of a snappy retort, but couldn't. In spite of herself she found herself smiling along with Boomer's joke.

"Hey, Boomer."

"Buy you lunch?"

They sat at a table for four by the front door in Laura's Restaurant. It was easy to tell the townfolk from the tourists simply by the way they looked at Boomer. The townfolk didn't stare. On the way in and out of the restaurant the local patrons stopped by their table and made small talk for a while. Their eyes met Boomer's then moved on to Cody's and Kim's. They looked at Boomer as one of their own who went away to protect them by serving their country and now was home.

The stares came from the tourists who only saw a young, scarred, disfigured man with misshapen hands.

The waitress brought out their deserts. As Boomer lifted his spoon a loud deep voice said, "What do we got here?" A black man as large as Boomer loomed over them.

Boomer said, "Aw jeez, they'll let anyone in here."

Garrett stood with his eyes taking in Boomer's face and hands, and then he paused as if thinking what to say next. Hovering and hidden behind Garrett was a child dressed in a Batman costume. The young boy peered around Garrett's immense leg and stared at Boomer.

Boomer pointed his spoon at the boy then shifted it to Garrett. "No way!"

"He's not my..." Garrett laughed. "He's my nephew." Garrett pulled out the chair next to Boomer then sat and gently swung the boy up in his lap. "Kellen, say hello to my friend, Boomer."

The young boy played with his mask trying to align the holes with his eyes. He seemed fascinated with Boomer.

He asked, "Where did you get your mask?"

Garrett said, "Kellen."

There was a long pause. No one at the table seemed to know how to fill the silence.

Boomer dug the spoon into the ice cream on top of his fudge brownie. "I got it in a place far, far away from here."

Kellen said, "It's pretty cool."

Boomer pushed his plate in front of the youngster.

"Can you help me eat this?"

The little boy turned and looked up at his uncle. Garrett nodded and the boy picked up the spoon.

CHAPTER 54

With Boomer home at least for a while, Cody thought he should get his own truck or maybe a car. He didn't really know which he preferred. Sometimes he felt like he was caught between two different worlds, but for now he wasn't going to decide. He figured he could hitch a ride with either Kim or Boomer. Anywhere he needed to go, he'd be with his two best friends.

After leaving town, Boomer wanted to take a ride along the river. Fall was Cody's favorite time of the year. Rich multicolored swaying leaves in the branches by the water cast a soothing hypnotic spell. For the first time in a long time, he relaxed. The tension and pressure of the football season was behind him. A soft resonance matched his feelings. It took a moment to realize that Boomer was whistling.

"Whoa!" said Boomer.

He braked and pulled over to the side of the two-lane road. "You see that!"

He shifted into reverse, then backed up with two wheels on asphalt and two on gravel. There was a "for sale" sign partially hidden by overgrown weeds.

"It's the old Shonebarger place."

Boomer spun the steering wheel, backed out on the road, then pulled into a narrow, gravel driveway.

Cody knew better than to ask what his brother was up to as he slowly drove forward. Trees lined the driveway, some so close they could reach out and touch them. Nestled under the trees on a bluff overlooking the river was a ranch house with a wrap-around porch. The white paint was peeling, half the shutters were hanging at odd angles, and the gutters were sagging.

Boomer put the truck in park.

"Come on, Little Bro."

He got out of the truck and walked up to the house.

What struck Cody first was the quiet. No town or city sounds - only the soft rustling of overhanging leaves. Boomer climbed up on the porch, then wiped one of the dirty windows trying to see inside.

"It's empty."

He tried the door.

"Locked."

Cody walked around the porch. There were screens on the windows on the river side. One of them was loose at the bottom. He pried the screen away from the window and set it on the porch. He pounded the frame, then smiled as he raised the unlocked window. He crawled through the window, then went and opened the front door for his brother.

"Check it out!" said Boomer.

The house was deceiving, larger on the inside than Cody thought it would be. The brothers set to work. Boomer stomped his foot to check the strength of the floorboards, then tapped his hands along the walls. Cody checked the three bedrooms. The air was stale with a layer of dust on the floor partially covering the wear marks from beds and dressers. There was a water stain on the ceiling of the largest room.

Boomer went to his truck and brought back a flashlight. He came inside and opened the trap door, then dropped down to the crawlspace under the house.

Cody checked the plumbing in the bathroom and kitchen. He could hear Boomer rummaging around under the floors. When he finished the inside, Cody went out and sat on the back steps and drew in deep, refreshing breaths.

"Whew!" Boomer came out the door wiping dirt from his knees and cobwebs from his hair. "She's solid, Little Bro." He plopped down next to his brother.

From the porch they had a clear view of the river below and the forest beyond. The way the sun lit the fall foliage was awesome. The cadence of rippling water soothed them as they sat, each lost in their own thoughts.

"The view's worth more than the house," Cody said.

"It's so peaceful."

Cody turned to his brother, surprised at the tone of his voice. Boomer got up from the porch and walked to the edge of the bluff, then looked back at the house.

As twilight approached, Cody put the screen back in, but left the window unlocked. They locked the front and back doors then walked out to the truck. About every 10 feet, Boomer stopped and turned back to gaze at the ranch house.

On the drive home, Boomer was quiet. Cody knew his brother well enough to know he was deep in thought, but he didn't know why.

CHAPTER 55

Thanksgiving was still weeks away, but Eileen couldn't wait. Both her boys were safely home under her roof and for her there was no greater cause to celebrate. The boys awoke to the aroma of a turkey roasting in the oven.

Cody stretched, then snuggled deeper under the blankets. No matter the weather, Boomer always slept with his window cracked open. From the hallway, crisp fall morning air slipped into his bedroom.

Boomer got out of bed and stomped to the bathroom. The vibrations were enough to awaken Cody's slumbering computer. The computer hummed and the screensaver appeared. It was a new picture. Gone was the image of Cody the quarterback standing in the pocket poised to throw a pass, replaced with the front page of the *Grand Rapids Gazette* with photos of Boomer past and present under Cody's and Kim's byline.

Cody always envied his brother because Boomer knew what he wanted to do with his life. Cody still wasn't sure what his future held, but he felt like he was getter closer. The story in the *Grand Rapids Gazette* made him realize that one person can make a difference. Knowing that he helped bring his brother home gave him feelings that he struggled to put into words, but it was a good struggle.

It was a traditional Thanksgiving dinner with all the trimmings. The table was set with sterling silver dinnerware handed down by Eileen's mother. Eileen gave up trying to shoo Boomer out of the kitchen as he snuck in to grab samples.

Kim came over early to help with the cooking. She wore a red dress which made Cody do a double-take again and again until Eileen wrapped her in a white apron.

Boomer seemed out of character. Since they left the Shonebarger place he was quiet, pensive. Cody still didn't know what was going on with his brother.

The family gathered around the table as Jack carved the large turkey. As he always did, he gave one of the legs to Boomer. Cody smiled as he remembered when he was a kid how he thought his brother looked like a Viking gnawing on the turkey leg.

When the plates were full, the family bowed their heads. Eileen led them in prayer. There was hardly any conversation during the meal - everyone was too consumed with the banquet set before them.

Coffee and desserts was the time for talk, for the family to catch up on all the past happenings and plans for the future. Jack, Eileen and Boomer sipped their coffees mixed with sighs of contentment. Kim came out of the kitchen carrying a tea set. She set a small cup and saucer in front of Cody then poured his tea. Cody glanced at his brother waiting for the sarcastic jab, but Boomer just smiled.

Boomer lifted his coffee cup with his right hand, his left hand with the missing fingers rested out of view in his lap.

He set the cup in the saucer and said, "The Shonebarger place is for sale."

Jack glanced at his wife knowing if anyone knew the comings and goings of Grand Rapids she would.

"George had a heart attack," said Eileen. "He died the week after Easter. Charlotte couldn't bear to stay in the house by herself. She's living with her daughter down in Atlanta."

"Why do you ask?" Jack said.

Boomer spun the coffee cup in circles on the saucer. "Cody and I were driving down by the river yesterday and I saw the "for sale" sign. We checked it out. You can tell no one's been living there for a while."

Knowing the answer before she asked, Eileen said, "You didn't go inside."

Boomer arched his eyebrows in a conspirator's gesture at Cody.

"The backdoor was open."

In a stern voice, Eileen said, "Boomer."

Boomer shrugged like it was no big deal.

"It needs a lot of work, but the foundation is solid. It's got a great view of the river." He glanced at Cody for confirmation. "It's just so peaceful."

Boomer paused and everyone waited for him to go on.

"I was thinking ... it'd be a nice place ... for Andy and some of the other guys to come and stay for a while." Boomer shook his head as he tried to put his thoughts into words. "It could be sort of like a halfway house for 'crispy critters' when they get out of the hospital. They could spend time by the river and then I could take them into town and let them get used to ..." His voice trailed off as he thought about taking Andy into Grand Rapids. "It would be a good place for him to start."

Boomer looked at his father. "It's a good house. You've always said, 'as long as the foundation is solid, we can rebuild it.'"

Boomer's words lingered over the dining room table. He glanced from face to face wondering why everyone was staring at him.

"What?"

"When do you want to start?" said Jack.

Boomer's eyes brightened. "Not tomorrow." He jabbed his finger at Cody. "I got plans for tomorrow." He looked back to his Dad. "How about the day after?"

CHAPTER 56

Carrying a woven wooden picnic basket, Kim lightly bounced down the steps from the upstairs living quarters to the photo shop. She set the basket on the counter next to her grandfather. With a flourish she opened the basket and took out a still-warm cinnamon roll.

Stanley laughed. "So that's what I've been smelling all morning."

Kim set the large white frosted roll on a plastic plate. "Do you have any idea how hard these are to make from scratch?"

Stanley lifted the roll and deeply inhaled. "Homemade. I haven't had one of these since I was a kid."

"Mrs. Brennan gave me her grandmother's recipe." Kim's eyes and lips tightened with nervous uncertainty as Stanley took a bite of the roll.

"Wow!" Stanley took another bite then licked the frosting from his lips. "This is incredible!"

Kim's eyes crinkled and her lips turned up in a smile. She felt like doing cartwheels.

"Maybe you should switch your major to home economics?"

She laughed. "No way."

Kim ducked behind the counter and lifted her camera, then swung it around her neck.

Stanley finished the roll and wiped his fingers on a napkin.

He asked, "Where are you off to?"

"To find the boys. They're playing hooky."

"Those two shouldn't be too hard to find."

Kim lifted another roll from the basket. Stanley started to protest as she set the roll on his plate.

He gave up and said, "I'll save it for later."

Kim tossed her sleek raven hair over her shoulder, then put on her baseball cap. She lifted the basket and her face filled with a happy, excited, can't wait to see what's around the next bend look.

Caught up in the moment, Stanley said, "Your mother would be so proud of you."

Kim paused feeling the words touch her. She set the basket down then went and hugged her grandfather.

The bells jingled as Kim opened the door to the photo shop. She walked out into bright fall sunshine, then closed the door behind her. Holding the basket, she stopped on the sidewalk and looked up and down her street. She knew she and Cody and Boomer had changed, but somehow Grand Rapids remained the same.

She set the basket on the back seat of her Honda, then opened the car's front door. She gazed back to her home. The white curtain upstairs fluttered. Her grandmother stood at the window. Kim waved, then got in her car and drove away.

CHAPTER 57

The water was cold but not as cold as it was during the spring thaw. Cody was wearing his waders. The brown swirling water was just above his knees. Boomer was out deeper in the river, the water at mid-thigh. The sun was almost directly overhead in a clear blue sky. They had been out for hours with hardly a nibble. Cody wasn't surprised or disappointed. The Walleyes wouldn't return until spring. Today, fishing was just time to unwind and be with his brother.

Boomer wore a floppy hat, sunglasses and gloves. He cast his line, then slowly pulled it back against the current. Downstream Buffalo Rock jutted up from the water not far from the Shonebarger ranch house on the bluff above the river.

The riverbank was lined with stately trees that had stood watch for centuries. The fall leaves were at their peak a kaleidoscope of yellows, burnt oranges and flaming reds above rich sienna soil.

Boomer reeled in his empty lure. Cody shrugged his shoulders in a 'what are you going to do gesture.' Boomer cast his line deeper into the river.

"You know ... I came here a thousand times," Boomer said.

Cody waded out closer to his brother so he could better hear him.

"I don't know how I did it, but when I was in the hospital
and things got really bad, somehow I would come here."

Cody nodded because he understood.

"And you were always here with me, Little Bro."

Cody couldn't find words to answer. He didn't know if it
was the sun or a shift in the current, but suddenly everything
felt warm.

Kim parked behind Boomer's truck on the bluff above the
river. The boys were knee deep in water fishing with their
backs to her. Thinking about Boomer, she couldn't help herself
as she pressed down on the horn. Both boys spun around. Cody
slipped on a rock. One arm went flailing as his other hand tried
to hold onto the fishing rod while he toppled backward.

"Whoa!" said Boomer. His right hand shot out and snatched
Cody's waders, then yanked him to his feet.

Kim laughed. She took the picnic basket from the back seat
and walked to the river. She yelled, "Yikes!" as she slid down
the embankment then jumped to the riverbank.

Cody burst out laughing at his escape from a sure drench-
ing. Boomer laughed along with him then waved at Kim who
set down the basket and lifted the camera.

"She's a keeper," Boomer said.

Cody's whole face smiled. He nodded, then threw his arm
around his brother's shoulder.

Kim took the picture.

ACKNOWLEDGMENTS

Dennis Bova for his editorial assistance and friendship

Karen for second chances